D0188640

WHAT IS THE SECRET?

July 18

Dear Diary,

This trip to London is finally beginning to show some hope. I put up with weak tea, stale cakes, and a couple of tedious old fogeys yesterday afternoon and my reward was a most interesting story. It seems the man who built the castle had a treasure. Something about the Civil War, though I can't imagine why an English duke cared about freeing slaves in America. Still, the man apparently knew jewels and precious metals. He also had a thing about horses. I could love someone like that. Anyway, it seems that nobody's ever found his treasure—until now, that is. I don't have time for all the details of what Mrs. Whatsername told me, but I know enough to know where to look. Won't that be a surprise to those goody-goodies, Lisa, Carole, and Stevie. I can't wait to see their faces when I find the treasure!

Veronica

Other Skylark Books you will enjoy
Ask your bookseller for the books you have missed

THE WINNING STROKE (American Gold Swimmers #1)
by Sharon Dennis Wyeth

COMPETITION FEVER (American Gold Gymnasts #1)
by Gabrielle Charbonnet

THE GREAT DAD DISASTER by Betsy Haynes

THE GREAT MOM SWAP by Betsy Haynes

BREAKING THE ICE (Silver Blades #1)

SAVE THE UNICORNS (Unicorn Club #1)

THEY'RE TORTURING TEACHERS IN ROOM 104
by Jerry Piasecki

WHAT IS THE TEACHER'S TOUPEE DOING
IN THE FISH TANK?
by Jerry Piasecki

THE SADDLE CLUB
SUPER #2

THE SECRET OF
THE STALLION

BONNIE BRYANT

A BANTAM SKYLARK BOOK
NEW YORK · TORONTO · LONDON · SYDNEY · AUCKLAND

I would like to express my special thanks to Dorothy Wood for her help and inspiration for this story. Your book on *The King's War* is finally on its way back to you!

BBH

RL 5, 009–012

THE SECRET OF THE STALLION
A Bantam Skylark Book / June 1995

Skylark Books is a registered trademark of Bantam Books,
a division of Bantam Doubleday Dell Publishing Group, Inc.
Registered in U.S. Patent and Trademark Office and elsewhere.

"The Saddle Club" is a registered trademark of Bonnie Bryant Hiller.
The Saddle Club design / logo, which consists of
a riding crop and a riding hat, is a
trademark of Bantam Books.

"USPC" and "Pony Club" are registered trademarks of
the United States Pony Clubs, Inc., at The Kentucky
Horse Park, 4071 Iron Works Pike, Lexington, KY 40511-8462.

All rights reserved.
Copyright © 1995 by Bonnie Bryant Hiller.
Cover art copyright © 1995 by Paul Casale.
No part of this book may be reproduced or transmitted
in any form or by any means, electronic or mechanical,
including photocopying, recording, or by any information
storage and retrieval system, without permission in
writing from the publisher.
For information address: Bantam Books.

If you purchased this book without a cover you should be aware that
this book is stolen property. It was reported as "unsold and destroyed"
to the publisher and neither the author nor the publisher has received
any payment for this "stripped book."

ISBN 0-553-48152-5

Published simultaneously in the United States and Canada

Bantam Books are published by Bantam Books, a division of Bantam Doubleday Dell Publishing Group, Inc. Its trademark, consisting of the words
"Bantam Books" and the portrayal of a rooster, is Registered in U.S. Patent
and Trademark Office and in other countries. Marca Registrada. Bantam
Books, 1540 Broadway, New York, New York 10036.

PRINTED IN THE UNITED STATES OF AMERICA

OPM   0   9   8

For Louisa

"WELCOME ABOARD FLIGHT Seven to London's Heathrow Airport."

"Can you believe that?" Stevie Lake asked, leaning over to her two best friends, Lisa Atwood and Carole Hanson. The three of them were seated next to one another on an airplane headed for London, England.

"I never thought this day would come!" Carole said.

"Me neither," agreed Lisa.

"Perhaps we'll have time for a spot of tea with the queen," Stevie said.

"Not likely," Carole said. "We're going to be much too busy worrying about how well we ride. We're not just here for fun, you know."

"Oh, but riding *is* fun," said Lisa. "And how could there be a better combination than being with my best friends, on an exciting trip, where we get to ride horses?"

"*. . . sure that your seat backs and tray tables are in their full upright and locked position prior to . . .*"

A face appeared above the seat in front of Lisa's. "Are you girls all buckled in?"

"Yes, Max," Stevie said. Max was Max Regnery, their riding instructor and one of their chaperons for the trip.

"Max, sit down yourself. Girls who can polish saddles as well as they can will certainly be able to manage to buckle a seat belt!"

That was Max's mother, the other half of the chaperon team. She was universally referred to as Mrs. Reg. Max and Mrs. Reg owned Pine Hollow Stables, where the girls rode. Mrs. Reg was the stable manager and occasional adviser to the girls.

The three girls were very different from one another. Carole was the most serious rider of the three. She'd been riding ever since she was a very little girl, starting with lessons on the Marine Corps bases where she'd lived all her life. Riding had always been the constant in Carole's life. When she was a child, her family had moved a lot, from base to base, but wherever she went, there were always horses. Now her father was a senior officer, a colonel, and was not likely to be moved any more before he retired from the Corps. Since her mother's death from cancer a few years earlier, Carole and her dad had lived alone in their house in the town of Willow Creek, not far from Quantico, where he worked.

Carole now had her own horse, Starlight, and she knew that no matter what else happened to her, horses would always be a major part of her life. When she grew up she would work with horses. Maybe she'd be a vet, maybe a trainer, maybe a championship rider, maybe a breeder. Maybe all of them. Horses were the one thing Carole never forgot. She might forget her own breakfast, but she'd never forget to feed Starlight. She might lose her own homework, but she'd never misplace Starlight's health records. She might forget to pack her bathrobe for a trip, but she'd never leave Starlight's blanket behind.

Carole wanted to learn everything there was to know about horses. She studied every book she had and she worked hard on all of her lessons at Horse Wise, the Pony Club at Pine Hollow. Whenever her friends weren't certain of something about horses, they knew they could ask Carole. Carole loved to share information, though sometimes her friends thought perhaps she shared too much. Stevie sometimes said that Carole gave twenty-five-cent answers to nickel questions.

Stevie contrasted sharply to Carole's seriousness. She loved horses just as much, but Stevie was much better known for her practical joking than she was for being serious. Often her practical jokes got her into trouble. Sometimes they got her friends into trouble, too. The good news was that she was almost as good at getting out of

trouble as she was at getting into it. Carole and Lisa usually groaned whenever Stevie came up with one of her
wild schemes, but, they had to admit, Stevie's schemes
sometimes got them into more fun than trouble. And,
sometimes they even worked.

Stevie's parents were both lawyers. She had three
brothers—one older, one younger, one twin. She was always scrapping with them and that got her into the worst
trouble because the boys never hesitated to scrap back.

In spite of Stevie's obstreperous, stubborn nature, she
was a very good rider. She was almost as good as Carole
and, in some forms, even better. Ironically, her strongest
skills lay in dressage, the most intricate form of riding
there was, requiring great concentration. What Stevie enjoyed about dressage exercises and tests was that it was
almost like a puzzle to her—a real challenge beyond the
normal demands of riding. Dressage was the ultimate test
of a horse's manners. The slightest shift in pressure or
weight by the rider should result in a proper response from
the horse. The well-trained horse and rider could do
amazing things in dressage. Stevie liked doing amazing
things. Stevie just recently got her own horse, an Arab-
Saddlebred mix named Belle. She loved working with
Belle on her training. "Work" wasn't the right word actually. Anything to do with horses was more like fun than
work.

It was a good thing for Stevie that she was disciplined
at riding because she was often just one step ahead of

detention at school. She was smart as could be, but she could be careless about school responsibilities and spent more time than the average student trying to explain things to Miss Fenton, the founder and director of Fenton Hall, the private school Stevie attended.

Lisa, on the other hand, was a straight-A student at Willow Creek Junior High School, where she and Carole went. She always did excellent work at school. She never forgot an assignment or waited until it was too late to complete a project. Stevie couldn't understand that part of Lisa at all. What she could understand was Lisa's love of horses.

Lisa had started riding only recently. But as with anything she tried, she was a good student and a fast learner. Max had often remarked that he'd never seen anyone learn so quickly. She was rightfully proud of that.

Lisa was logical and methodical. Her mother had seen to it that she'd developed many skills in her thirteen years. She'd had dance classes (ballet, tap, *and* ballroom), music lessons, painting lessons, tennis lessons, sewing classes, and drama classes. Most of those had stopped, however, when Lisa discovered horses. Her mother had thought that every proper young lady should know something about horses. Lisa disagreed there. After one lesson, she didn't want to know *something* about horses. She wanted to know *everything* about horses.

That was how she'd met up with Stevie and Carole. And that was when the three of them, different as they were, discovered that they had one thing in common that was much more important than everything about them that was different: They were horse-crazy. So they'd started The Saddle Club. It only had two rules. Members had to be horse-crazy and they had to be willing to help one another.

The girls had riding classes on Tuesdays and Horse Wise Pony Club meetings on Saturdays. They usually found excuses to get to Pine Hollow other days as well. Their hard work and focus on horses and riding had earned them the respect of Max Regnery.

That, in turn, had earned them the right to be on the airplane that had now taken off and was flying over the Atlantic Ocean to London. They were going to England as part of an international Pony Club exchange program. Sometime earlier the program had brought four dashing and fun Italian boys to Willow Creek, Virginia. Now The Saddle Club was going to perform in a mounted games demonstration of Pony Clubbers at a three-day event in England.

"How long are we staying in London?" Carole asked.

"Three days," said Lisa. "That should give us a chance to see a few things, though not nearly as many as my parents dragged me to when we were there for two weeks last summer." She consulted the itinerary Mrs. Reg's travel agent had prepared for everyone. Stevie had had one, but couldn't find it in her backpack. Carole had left hers at home. "Then we take a chartered bus to Cummington Castle, where the three-day event takes place."

"I can't wait for the three-day event," said Carole. "A full day of dressage, followed by one of endurance cross-country riding, and finishing up with stadium jumping. Did you know that three-day events were originally devised to test a military horse's fitness at charging in battle? The difficulty of the program would test any horse's fitness, actually, but it gave the officers a chance to show off their horses' courage and endurance as well. The three-day event was originally called a Military. Did you know that?"

"I do now," said Lisa. She was always interested in what Carole had to share, but if she and Stevie didn't stop her, Carole would get into a lengthy history of the event that might not stop until they touched down at Heathrow!

Stevie tugged on Max's seat back to get his attention. "Is it true that Nigel is going to be there?" she asked.

"That's what Dorothy said," Max told her through the space between the seats. Dorothy was a former student of Max's, now retired from showing because of a riding accident. She was married to Nigel Hawthorne, a member of the British Equestrian Team. It seemed quite logical that he would be competing in a prestigious event like Cummington. "Didn't I tell you about the horse he'll be riding?"

No, he hadn't, and the girls told him so.

"He's riding a stallion by the name of Pound Sterling. He's from Yawelkesleigh Farms."

"Yaw-what?" asked Stevie.

"I don't know how to pronounce it—just how to spell it, and I'm not so sure of that," said Max. "Anyway, Dorothy was excited about the horse. Said Nigel would bring out the best in the animal."

Of that, there was no doubt. Nigel was a wonderful rider, and the girls were really excited about having the chance to cheer for him.

"I'm going to sleep now and I suggest you do the same," Max said. He reached up and switched off his light. "We'll be in London before you know it, and we've got a long day ahead of us."

The girls didn't switch off their lights and they had no intention of going to sleep. There was much too much to talk about.

"Are you sure Tessa is going to be there?" Carole asked Lisa.

Lisa reached into her purse again and pulled out the letter she'd received from Lady Theresa, better known to her as Tessa. Lisa had met Tessa when she'd been in England with her parents. She was an actual, true titled English lady and a distant cousin to the queen, but as far as Lisa was concerned, the most important thing about Tessa was that she was just a really nice girl about Lisa's own age.

Lisa opened the letter. "Yup, here it is. She writes, 'I can't wait to see you. I have some wonderful fun planned for us all. Do save a day for me. Will you and your friends be able to come riding at our place?'"

"You did say yes, didn't you?" Stevie asked.

"You think I'm crazy? Of course I said yes!"

"Did anyone hear from the Italian boys?" Carole asked.

"Not me," said Lisa.

"Max did," Stevie told her friends. "He heard from their coach anyway. They'll be there—all four of them. Remember how much fun we had when Enrico, Marco, Gian, and Andre were at Pine Hollow?"

Carole turned to Lisa. "And you saw Enrico when you were in Italy with your parents, didn't you?"

"I sure did. We stayed with him, in their house."

"Didn't you say it was more like a castle?" Stevie asked.

"I guess it was," Lisa agreed. "It seemed to me that it was so big that the East Wing had a West Wing."

"I never would have figured him for a zillionaire," said Stevie. "He's so normal."

"Just being rich doesn't make someone a snob," Lisa said.

"Speaking of that, I wonder how Veronica is doing," said Stevie. She was referring to Veronica diAngelo, another rider at Pine Hollow and the fourth member of their relay team. She was on the same plane they were on. She was just in another section.

9

July 15

Dear Diary,

Thank goodness for first class!

When Max and Mrs. Reg, Stevie, Lisa, and Carole were getting into their seats back in coach, I saw how jammed they were. I also got a whiff of the food they were going to have to eat! At least my parents had the good sense to put me in the front of the plane. And Daddy promised he'd ordered a car service to take me to the hotel. I'll have my cases unpacked by the time the others get off the bus, and I'll be sound asleep before they get checked in.

I've finished the caviar and other hors d'oeuvres. While the attendant is grilling my steak, I thought I'd take a minute to write in my journal. I'll be going to sleep right after dinner. These wide seats are so comfortable!

And they'd better be to make up for what Daddy asked me to do. He says I have to call these people, the Chumleys. Can you believe the name? Anyway, it seems like they are some kind of big important client of Daddy's bank.

Well, if it's so important to Daddy, I guess I can do it. I just hope I don't have to spend any time with them or anything. There are too many wonderful stores to visit in London for me to want to waste any time with some old fuddy-duddies.

Here comes the steak! Good night—

Veronica

2

"IF SHE SAYS one more word about how good her steak was, I think I'm going to throttle her," Stevie grumbled to Lisa. They were all standing in a line at Heathrow.

"Have you seen my passport?" Carole asked Lisa.

"Who has the luggage claims?" Max asked.

"Did you girls sleep at all?" asked Mrs. Reg.

"Who cares? It's in your left hand. Mrs. Reg has them. And no," Lisa said, addressing everybody's concerns at once. It was eight o'clock in the morning and her body thought it was the middle of the night, but Lisa could still be organized and everybody knew they could count on her. Even Veronica followed her as the group stood waiting to have their passports stamped.

"What comes next?" Stevie asked.

"Luggage claim," Lisa said authoritatively.

"I think we should always travel with her," Max teased. "She knows everything. I'm still half asleep."

"Oh, really?" Veronica said, sounding surprised. "Didn't you sleep well?"

Max didn't answer. He did, however, put his arm out to keep Stevie from throttling Veronica, who had spent the five minutes since they'd met at the door of the plane telling the others how nice first class was.

Lisa collected their passports and presented them to the immigration officer all at once.

"Business or pleasure?" he asked.

"Business," said Max.

"Pleasure," said The Saddle Club.

"We're going to be riding horses," Carole explained.

"Have a good visit," said the officer, stamping their passports.

Fifteen minutes later, they had found their luggage and passed through customs. Now all they had to do was find transportation into the city.

"Daddy's ordered a car service for me," said Veronica. "If you want, a few of you could come along, though it won't be much fun if it's crowded . . ."

It was an invitation that did not endear Veronica to her fellow travelers.

"No thanks," Stevie said. "We'll manage in tourist. You just go ahead in first class."

"Oh, all right," said Veronica, apparently oblivious to the irritation she was causing.

They took their bags out to the curb.

A long, shiny black limousine pulled up near where they stood. Veronica's eyes lit up in expectation. The door opened. Out jumped a girl about the age of The Saddle Club's members. She had a big grin on her face and she waved wildly, trying to get their attention.

"Lisa! Lisa, it's me!"

Lisa turned. "Tessa! You came to meet us?"

"Of course!" The girls ran to meet one another and hugged. "And there's plenty of room in this boat of a car for everyone, plus bags. Hamilton," she said to the driver, "can you help them stow the luggage in the boot?"

Hamilton tipped his hat and the trunk lid slid open. He started taking suitcases.

As Stevie handed her bag to Hamilton, she looked at Veronica. Veronica was still waiting for the car service her father had ordered, looking impatiently over the sea of cars and taxis. Then it came.

A small, once red car that looked as if it had seen better days—many of them—pulled up to the curb. A scruffy, unshaven man stepped out. He pulled a piece of cardboard out with him. It said "diAngelo" on it. He spotted the group from Pine Hollow and walked over, partly in response to a wave from Stevie.

"Miz doy Hangelo?" he asked Stevie in a very thick accent she assumed was what the English called Cockney.

13

"No, not I," said Stevie. "This is Miss diAngelo." She pointed to the pale Veronica.

"Royt this whoy, miss," he said, picking up Veronica's suitcase. She had nothing to do but follow him. The look on her face as she headed to the old beat-up car while her friends climbed into a spacious limousine was worth every bite of soggy pizza that Stevie had suffered while cramped in the economy section of the airplane. Stevie sighed with contentment.

None of the group started laughing until after the limousine's doors had shut and the windows had been raised. Then even Max couldn't contain himself.

They agreed that they would be sure to call her "Miz doy Hangelo" only on very special occasions.

A FEW HOURS later, The Saddle Club felt like different people. They'd had a chance to check into their hotel, unpack a few things, and take a nap. They were refreshed and ready to see the world by noon when Tessa showed up to take them on the grand tour.

Again Hamilton was there with the car. The girls invited Veronica to join them, knowing she wouldn't be able to resist the limousine. Stevie thought it was too bad that Veronica was so impressed with Tessa's car that Veronica never seemed to notice what a nice person Tessa was. That was just like Veronica, too.

"First stop—the Tower of London," said Tessa.

They took off.

The Tower was an old castle in the center of what was now London's business district—like Wall Street in New York. It had stood on the banks of the Thames River (Tessa pronounced it "the Tems") for a thousand years. Kings and queens had been beheaded there, and nobody knew how many had suffered torture and death in its infamous dungeon.

"This place gives me the creeps," said Carole.

"Me too. Isn't it wonderful?" Stevie remarked.

"Can you imagine all the history this place has seen?" Lisa sighed.

"Where are the crown jewels?" Veronica wanted to know.

They saw the creepy parts, the wonderful ones, the historic places, and, of course, the crown jewels. It gave them all a start to realize that, as even a distant cousin to the queen, Tessa was probably related to some of the people who had ruled, and suffered, within the walls of the Tower of London.

"*Very* distant relatives," Tessa explained, laughing.

Even Veronica couldn't resist laughing when Tessa said silly things like that.

Their next stop was Madame Tussaud's Wax Museum. It was a collection of wax statues, very real likenesses, of famous people, all dressed in costumes of their times. In some cases, like the one of Elvis Presley, the wax statues were wearing clothes that had actually belonged to the real people.

15

"Oh, look at the gowns!" Veronica remarked, admiring some of the clothes the wax royals were wearing.

"I don't know," said Stevie. "In some ways, this is creepier than the Tower of London. At least there, I could just imagine the people. Here, I have to see them—in wax."

Carole sat down on a seat next to another tired tourist. A second look at her seatmate revealed that it was actually another wax statue! She laughed and called her friends over.

"Maybe they'll make statues of us to put in here someday. We wouldn't take up much space, would we?" she asked.

"I don't think they're interested in American riders here," said Tessa. "They mostly want the famous, the infamous, and the gory—"

"Preferably all three," Stevie said, passing by a gruesome dungeon scene.

"This stuff turns my stomach," said Lisa.

"My *empty* stomach," said Stevie.

"You know, until you mentioned it, I didn't realize how hungry I was," said Carole. "The last real meal we had was that soggy pizza they served us for dinner." She glared at Veronica so she wouldn't say anything about the steak she'd had on the plane.

"Well, then, how about some *good* pizza?" Tessa asked. "There's this wonderful little place . . ."

She didn't have to say it twice. The American girls

16

followed her gladly to the limousine. Hamilton drove them to Tessa's favorite pizza restaurant.

They gathered at the table, placed their orders, and talked about plans for the rest of their visit to London.

"Tomorrow you're all going to come to our home and ride with me, aren't you?"

"Yes!" came three enthusiastic responses.

"I'm afraid I can't," came the fourth. The girls looked at Veronica. "It's these friends of Daddy's," she explained. "I called them as soon as I checked into my room and they've invited me to tea at their home. They live in Mayfair . . ."

She let the word "Mayfair" hang in the air. It suggested so much. It suggested wealth and glamour, country estates, and very blue blood. It was just a word, but Veronica had managed to pack a whole world into that one word.

"How nice for you," said Tessa. She sounded as if she meant it, too.

"Yes," said Stevie. "How nice." She didn't sound as if she meant it.

Veronica smiled and took a bite of pizza. A gob of gooey, greasy cheese slid off the top of the pizza and landed on her lap. Everyone handed her a napkin. Nobody helped her clean the mess.

17

AFTER A VERY good night's sleep, the three American girls had been picked up by Hamilton and driven to Tessa's country home. It wasn't far from London. The trip was only about forty-five minutes, but they had a good look at the lovely green countryside that surrounded the city.

They'd followed signs to a town named Harcourt-St. Claire's-in-the-Wold, which Hamilton referred to as Hart-Sinclair. That struck Stevie as a neat way to get rid of a lot of extraneous syllables.

As they drove they chatted nervously about their hostess, Tessa's mother.

"I've never been to a lady's home before," said Stevie. "I'm going to do something awful and be an embarrassment to every American. I don't even know how to hold a teacup."

"Just don't crook your little finger," said Carole.

"How do you know?" asked Lisa.

"Veronica told me," said Carole.

"I guess we can count on that, then," said Stevie. She practiced holding a teacup without crooking her little finger. Instead she stuck it straight out in the air.

"No, not like that, either. Just hold it normally," said Carole.

"You mean like regular people? But Tessa's mother is a lady!"

"So's Tessa," Lisa reminded her. "And she's normal, isn't she?"

Stevie thought about that while the sleek, black limousine turned into a long drive and then to a circle in front of a big old stone house that Tessa had called Dickens.

Tessa came running out of the house to greet the girls. Her mother followed, with a welcoming smile that immediately put the girls at ease.

"Come on in, then, and change your clothes for your ride," said the woman. "You're to go have yourselves a good ride and then come back here for lunch. I've made a special treat for our American visitors."

Everybody was introduced, and within a half hour the four girls were in the saddle.

"I can't believe it!" said Stevie. "I'm actually riding on

an English horse, with an English lady, in the English countryside! Pinch me!"

"I would, but somebody needs to pinch *me* first," said Carole.

"This way!" said Tessa. Lisa, Carole, and Stevie followed. "I'll show you all around Hart-Sinclair—the only way to see it, on horseback."

Stevie's horse lunged forward eagerly, and she was only too happy to let him have his head. He was an energetic sorrel named Copperfield after *David Copperfield*. All of the horses at Dickens were named after characters in Charles Dickens's novels. Lisa was riding Pip, a gray. Carole's horse, a chestnut mare, was named Miss Havisham. Those were both names of characters from *Great Expectations*. Tessa's own horse was named Humbug after Scrooge's favorite exclamation in *A Christmas Carol*. Everything at Dickens was even nicer and more fun than Stevie and her friends could have imagined.

VERONICA FROWNED ONE final time before she reached for the bell at the Chumleys' house. She was not happy to be there and she was going to be sure her father knew that she'd missed a chance to ride at Dickens in Hart-Sinclair. Perhaps he'd find a tangible way to express his gratitude to her—like a new saddle.

Veronica pressed the button. A maid answered and requested her name. She was invited inside and asked to wait in the sitting room. She sat and waited.

The sitting room was dark and grand. The walls held oil portraits of what she suspected were generations of Chumleys. There was a strong jawline that seemed to appear in most of the generations. It wasn't a very attractive strong jawline, just a strong jawline. Veronica wondered if anybody famous had done any of the paintings. The furniture was old, too. Veronica wondered if any of it was Chippendale. The rugs were oriental. Perhaps they were valuable, too. Maybe this wouldn't be so bad after all.

The door opened. Mr. and Mrs. Chumley walked in slowly. Veronica's first thought was that they were old. Her second thought was that they were *very* old. Mr. Chumley used a cane. Mrs. Chumley squinted through her glasses, trying to focus on Veronica. Veronica stood up and shook their frail old hands as she knew her father would expect her to do. She smiled as she knew her father would expect her to do. She told them how pleased she was to see them. But all she could think of was how much she wished she were at Hart-Sinclair. Even being with Stevie, Lisa, and Carole was better than this.

"Edna, bring the tea, won't you?" Mrs. Chumley asked the maid. "And those nice little almond cakes?"

They sat.

Veronica smiled again. "Daddy will be so pleased that I'm having a chance to meet you," she said.

Mr. Chumley jutted his strong jaw forward and leaned toward Veronica. His bushy white mustache quivered as he began to form his words.

21

"Who's that?" he asked.

"M-My father," Veronica stammered.

"Mr. diAngelo—from the bank in Virginia, dear. Remember him?" said Mrs. Chumley.

"DiAngelo, diAngelo," said the old man. "Can't say as I do." He sat back in his chair.

"Of course you do, Alastair," said Mrs. Chumley. "And this is their daughter, Jessica."

"Veronica," said Veronica.

"Of course, Veronica," agreed Mrs. Chumley.

The tea arrived. Veronica smiled wanly as Mrs. Chumley assembled a cup of tea and an almond cake on a plate for her. Her eyes were on Mrs. Chumley, but her mind was somewhere else: Harcourt-St. Claire's-in-the-Wold. She swore to herself that her friends would never, ever, in their entire lives know what a ghastly time she was having with the Chumleys. She blinked back a tear.

"Tell me, Je—I mean Veronica," Mrs. Chumley said, "just what it is you're doing here."

"Visiting you," said Veronica. "You invited me for tea, remember?"

"You mean you came all the way to England from Virginia for our almond cakes?" Mr. Chumley asked.

"No, dear," Mrs. Chumley said to her husband. Then she turned to Veronica. "Actually, I knew I'd invited you to tea. What I meant was that I can't recall why it is you came to England."

"Horses," said Veronica. "I'm a rider. My Pony Club is

doing a mounted games demonstration at a three-day event in Cummington."

"Oh, of course, the Cummington," said Mrs. Chumley.

"You've heard of it?" Veronica asked, unable to keep the surprise from her voice.

"Naturally. Everybody has," said Mrs. Chumley. "And I do hope you'll have a chance to see the ghost while you're there."

"The ghost?" Veronica asked. This whole tea party was acquiring the most surreal quality!

"The duke's ghost, of course. To protect the treasure, don't you know."

"The treasure?" said Veronica.

"Is there an echo in here?" asked Mr. Chumley.

"Oh, hush, Alastair," said Mrs. Chumley. "It's just our American visitor. She doesn't know about the buried treasure at Cummington Castle."

"So, why don't you tell her?" Mr. Chumley suggested. That was the first and only time that afternoon when he said anything that made sense to Veronica.

"Indeed I shall," said Mrs. Chumley.

Veronica took a bite out of her almond cake and a sip of tea. She put her cup and plate on the table and sat up expectantly. She didn't want to miss a thing.

CAROLE GAVE MISS Havisham a final hug. "You've been a wonderful horse to ride and I wish I could ride you again," she whispered in the horse's ear.

23

"Isn't she a dream?" Tessa said.

"She was great," Carole agreed. "She was especially good at fast starts and stops. I kept thinking how good she'd be in mounted games, like the ones we'll be demonstrating at Cummington."

"I had the same thought about Pip," Lisa said. "He could turn on a dime."

"You should say seven pence," Stevie interjected. "We're in England now and they have different money. A dime is somewhere between six and seven p, I think."

"I know what a dime is," Tessa said. "I also knew what she meant. Pip is very maneuverable."

"But he's not as fast as Copperfield," Stevie said. "Copperfield'd beat anybody in a race, I'm sure."

"So you all liked your horses?" Tessa asked.

"Yes," came three enthusiastic responses.

"Then you'll probably be glad to know that I've arranged for you to ride this lot at Cummington. I couldn't stand the idea of you having to take whatever old horse nobody else wanted for your demonstration. They're being driven to the castle tomorrow and will be waiting for you there."

"You what?" Stevie asked.

"I told you she was wonderful, didn't I?" asked Lisa.

"Yes, but you didn't say she was *this* wonderful," said Carole.

"I'm sending another horse, a dappled gray named Nickleby, for the other girl—what's her name?"

24

"Veronica," Lisa supplied.

"Right. Well, Nickleby's a jolly good horse, too."

The Saddle Club couldn't believe how wonderful and generous Tessa was being and they told her so. She explained that she had the horses and the van and the driver and, since she was planning to be at Cummington to cheer them on, they were going to have to do well and the best way to be assured of that was to provide them with good mounts. It was all as logical as it was wonderful.

The girls finished grooming and watering their horses and packed their tack for the trip to Cummington. They each delivered a final hug to their horses and then returned to the main house for lunch.

"I wonder what your mother has cooked up for us," Stevie said, sniffing the air suspiciously.

"It smells good," said Carole.

"It smells familiar," said Lisa.

"It smells like pizza," said Tessa. "She thinks it's the most American food there is and I guess she decided that would be what you'd want. Isn't that funny? Well, can you stand pizza two days in a row?"

They all smiled enthusiastically. Nobody told Tessa's mother that it was more like three days in a row because it had been dinner on the airplane, too.

THE NEXT MORNING, Lisa edged through the crowd. She didn't want to miss a thing.

Carole heard it first. "They're coming!" she said. She turned to look. So did several thousand other people.

"Look!" said Stevie, standing on her toes. "There are the horses!"

The crowd strained against the barriers as the horse guards approached Buckingham Palace.

There were perhaps forty mounted guards, dressed in bright red uniforms and smart caps with feathers fluttering in the warm summer breeze. The guards rode four abreast down the Mall toward the palace, heads forward, eyes straight ahead. The horses clopped along the paved street in near unison, in much the same way they must have done for hundreds of years.

All around cameras clicked. The tourists crowded for a better look.

"Don't miss the picture! Bert! Get a picture!" one lady shouted at her husband as he tried to load film into his camera.

"Did you see the one flinch? Did you get that with the videocam?" a father said excitedly to his son.

"Look at all those horses! They must be identical twins!" uttered a little girl.

Stevie, Lisa, Carole, and Veronica watched, too. They were more interested in the horses than in the guards. The girls admired the way the riders handled the turns. When four horses marching abreast came to a turn, the ones on the outside had to turn farther and faster than the ones on the inside to keep the formation from becoming straggly. Not surprisingly, these riders executed the turns with military perfection.

"Nice!" said Stevie. She was always particularly aware of good technique in intricate riding.

"They take wonderful care of the horses," said Carole. "Every one of them is perfectly groomed."

"And did you see how the tack gleamed in the sun?" asked Mrs. Reg.

The girls all giggled when she said that. Mrs. Reg was famous for finding people to polish tack. "Nothing like supple leather," she'd say.

27

"It's very supple," said Lisa. That made her friends giggle. Even Max smiled.

"Nobody respects me," Mrs. Reg said. But she was teasing and the girls knew it. They respected her a lot and there was a good deal of gleaming leather at Pine Hollow to attest to that fact.

The guards entered the palace grounds and proceeded through an old ritual, replacing old guards with new as the shift changed.

The performance was executed perfectly and the crowd appreciated it. Within weeks, thousands of photographs of the event would be placed lovingly in albums all around the world. Lisa tucked her camera back into its case, hoping her pictures would come out.

When the last guard was in place and the last photograph had been taken, Mrs. Reg invited everybody to take a walk.

"Are we going near Harrods?" Veronica asked. Harrods was London's very famous, and very expensive, department store. Veronica could hardly wait to get there.

"Not really, dear. I was planning a stroll through the parks. This one here, to our right, is Green Park."

"Isn't that a silly name for a park?" Veronica said grumpily. "Isn't that the point of parks—to be green?"

"Then it seems like an utterly sensible name for a park," said Mrs. Reg matter-of-factly.

She led the group into the park. The paths were pleasant and wide. On the lawn, many people were enjoying the day, sitting quietly, talking, or playing games. A group of children played something that looked a bit like football.

"Rugby," Max said. "Some people would disagree with this definition, but it's something like a cross between what we call soccer and the English call football, and our football, which the English call American football." Stevie didn't care what it was called. She thought it looked like fun.

They came to an enormous traffic circle, which Mrs. Reg explained the English called a roundabout.

"Everything's the same, but everything's different," Stevie said, thinking out loud. "A traffic circle's a roundabout; a car trunk is a boot; an elevator is a lift; and soccer is football, but football is American football. It's all very strange."

Max laughed. "England and America have been described as 'two nations divided by a common language,'" he told them. It seemed to be true.

They made it across the roundabout by going underground through a series of tunnels and emerged at a place Mrs. Reg told them was called Hyde Park Corner.

"This way," said Max.

They left the corner and followed him into Hyde Park. To their right was a large open area where some boys were flying kites. To their left was Rotten Row.

"What's rotten about it?" Veronica asked.

"Nothing at all," said Carole, a grin crossing her face. "Because look, this is where people ride horses."

The approach of hoofbeats told everybody she was right. The whole group turned to see the approaching horses. It was more than a little bit comforting to see such a familiar sight in such an unfamiliar place. What they weren't prepared for was exactly how familiar the sight was going to be.

"It's the Italians!" said Stevie.

"Marco! Gian! Enrico! Andre!" Carole cried.

Lisa waved at them; so did Max and Mrs. Reg. Veronica took a moment to smooth her skirt.

The four boys drew to a halt in front of the astonished Americans.

"But what are you doing here?" Marco asked.

"Waiting for you," Stevie teased.

"How wonderful!" said Andre.

"Lisa! How have you been?" asked Enrico.

"I've been fine," Lisa said. She was pleased to see Enrico and remembered what a wonderful time she and her parents had had visiting his home when they were in Italy. "We all have. We're just excited to be here and we can't wait to go to Cummington tomorrow. What are you doing now, practicing for the mounted games?"

"Hardly," Enrico said. "We can't really do that here and it wouldn't do much good unless these were the horses we'll be riding in the games. However, our coach thought it would be good for us to stay in shape, so he

30

hired these fellows for us. Mine has been giving me trouble all day."

Lisa took the horse's reins near his mouth and patted his neck while she talked with Enrico.

"Sometimes horses just get moody, don't they?" she asked. It had happened to her enough that she knew it was true.

"Yes indeed. I just wish this one wouldn't be moody when I'm in the saddle."

The horse flinched. Lisa gripped the reins a little more tightly. It wasn't that Enrico wasn't also holding the reins; he was. It was more that she was closer to the horse's mouth, where a little tug might have a more immediate effect.

"My mother keeps talking about you," Enrico said. "I was told about twenty times to 'say hello to that nice American girl, Lisa, and her parents.'"

"That's funny," said Lisa. "My mother told me to be sure to tell you again how much we all enjoyed staying with you in Italy."

"And you?" Enrico asked. The tone of his voice had changed. It was quieter, more personal and somehow urgent. "Did you enjoy it, too?"

"Oh, yes," she said, almost breathless, realizing for the first time that Enrico really liked her.

She looked up at him sitting in the saddle, his head silhouetted against the bright sky. And then she saw something that Enrico didn't see. A kite suddenly soared

31

across the sky, skittering down to the earth not two feet from where she and Enrico stood. It was more than Enrico's fidgety horse could stand. He couldn't run because Enrico had the reins. He couldn't rear because Lisa held his bit. But he could buck. And buck he did. Enrico had no warning at all. He flew right over the horse's head, did a somersault, and landed on his rear!

Lisa was so astonished she barely knew what to do first. Max came to the rescue. Max took the horse's reins from her hand and separated him from the group until he was back under control.

Lisa ran to Enrico and knelt next to him. He pulled himself up to a sitting position.

"Are you all right?" she asked. "Enrico? Can you see me? Is anything broken? Are you hurt? Can you stand up?"

He fluttered his eyes. Then he whispered weakly to her. She had to lean forward to hear him.

"I'm sure I can stand up, Lisa, but as long as you're willing to take care of me, I think I'll stay right where I am." There was a totally irresistible twinkle in his eyes.

Lisa burst into laughter and stood up. She offered Enrico a hand, and he stood up as well.

Mrs. Reg asked him if he was okay, and he gave her a much more serious answer than he'd given Lisa, assuring her that he was fine. By then, Max had calmed the horse down. The bay gelding was no longer fussing and fidgeting.

"I think he's okay to ride, but I'm not certain," said Max. "I'd be uncomfortable having you get back on him again. Are the stables far away?"

"Not really," Marco told Max. "We were on our way back there when we spotted you."

"Then why don't I ride with you boys and we'll return the horses and meet the rest of you someplace for lunch. Any suggestions?"

"I have an idea," said Enrico. "We saw a lot of restaurants over by Piccadilly Circus, including a pizza place. Andre, Marco, Gian, and I were remembering the wonderful American pizza you girls gave us in Virginia. Perhaps you'd let us buy you some English pizza today, and then in the future we'll have real Italian pizza—"

"Wonderful," said Max. "The last pizza I had was that revolting stuff on the plane. Mother, why don't you take Enrico and the girls there. The boys and I will meet you there in about as much time as it will take them to make two large pizzas!"

How could the girls say no to such a gracious invitation? Mrs. Reg pulled out her map and guide book and pointed to the right.

"Piccadilly's straight ahead!" She led. They followed.

* * *

Dear Mom & Daddy,

Saw the Chumleys yesterday. Did the tea thing. They live in a dusty old house stuffed to the gills with antiques. Not surprising they're important clients, but, Daddy, I missed riding at Dickens House with Lady Theresa to see those fogeys. CAN YOU BELIEVE IT'S BEEN THREE YEARS SINCE I GOT A NEW SADDLE????

Just back from Buckingham Palace—the changing of the guard. How quaint! How touristy! Tomorrow I think I'll get to Harrods—finally! And then to the castle in the afternoon. Sounds like an interesting place, though I doubt there's much good shopping in the town of Cummington.

Love,
Veronica

July 18

Dear Diary,

This trip is finally beginning to show some hope. For the longest time, I thought it would simply be eight days of tolerating The Saddle Club in order to have some fun in London and have the opportunity of meeting some people more my class in Cummington, but there have been a few developments that make the whole trip more promising than I could have imagined.

First, there's the castle. I put up with weak tea, stale cakes, and a couple of tedious old fogeys yesterday afternoon and my reward was a most interesting story. It seems the man who built the castle had a treasure. Something about the Civil War, though I can't imagine why an English duke cared about freeing slaves in America. Still, the man apparently knew jewels and precious metals. He also had a thing about horses. I could love someone like that. Anyway, it seems that nobody's ever found his treasure—until now, that is. I don't have time for all the details of what Mrs. Whatsername told me, but I know enough to know where to look. Won't that be a surprise to those goody-goodies, Lisa, Carole, and Stevie. I can't wait to see their faces when I find the treasure!

I also can't wait to see the face of one of them in particular when she discovers that a certain boy who thinks he's interested in her finds out that I have a lot more to offer than she does. He'll drop her in a minute when he learns how common she is. And the beauty of it is that I'll be right there when he starts to look around again. I won't have to lift a finger—all I have to do is to be there.

Tomorrow I'll see the inside of some of London's better stores—or I'll scream. I just have this urge to shop!

Veronica

5

"WHAT'S *THIS?*" VERONICA asked the next morning at breakfast. She was looking at a bowl of viscous hot cereal that the waitress had put in front of her.

"Porridge," Lisa told her. "It's part of breakfast every morning here at the hotel. Didn't you notice?"

"Hardly," said Veronica. She handed the bowl to a passing waitress and concentrated on the bread and tea.

"Speaking of tea, Veronica," Stevie said. "How was your visit with that friend of your family the other day?"

Veronica pasted a smile on her face. She'd promised herself that these girls would never know the truth about that visit—any of it.

"Delightful," Veronica said. "Such a cute old couple!

36

Daddy was absolutely right. I found them totally charming. Too bad you three had to be dragged way out into the country. I'm sure you would have loved the Chubbles."

"Wasn't their name Chumley?" Stevie asked. She considered Veronica's enthusiasm highly suspicious.

"Chumley—whatever. Anyway I'm sorry you couldn't be there with me." With that, she tossed a half-eaten roll onto her breakfast plate and stood up.

"I'm going to change to go shopping this morning. Anyone else interested in going to Knightsbridge?"

The girls had learned enough about London to know that Knightsbridge was a major shopping area. That's where Harrods was, as well as a number of London's other fine stores and exclusive shops—the kind of place that Veronica liked best.

"We're going to the Science Museum," said Stevie. "At least that's what Carole and I were talking about with a couple of the Italian boys. Are you coming, too?" she asked Lisa.

Lisa finished the last bite of her porridge. "I don't think so," she said. "Enrico said he thought it would be fun just to walk around. I think that's what we're going to do. Max said we could do whatever we wanted as long as we had maps and promised to be back here for the bus at one, right?"

"Right," Carole said.

"Well, I'll see you a little later," said Veronica, finally leaving the girls alone in the breakfast room.

"She *hated* the Chumleys!" Stevie hissed victoriously to her friends.

"She is *so* transparent!" said Lisa.

"Like glass," Carole agreed. "But the best part about that is that she has to keep on pretending we really missed something, when we know that she knows that *she's* the one who missed something great by not riding at Dickens with Tessa."

"When I learned that Veronica was coming on this trip with us, I thought it was all bad news," Stevie said. "Now it turns out that it's almost the most fun of all. Here she is in England, a place that people think is sort of snobbish, but as far as I'm concerned isn't at all that way, and we've got the biggest American snob of all with us and she's having a miserable time. Isn't life grand?"

"Totally," Lisa agreed.

"Naturally you'd say that," said Carole. "Because you've got this incredibly rich Italian boy positively drooling over you. Personally, I think it's, it's . . ." She searched for a word. *"Wonderful!"*

"Me too," Lisa agreed.

Stevie clapped Lisa on the back enthusiastically. "Have fun," she said.

"I will—that is if I can keep Veronica out of our hair. She seems to want to follow me wherever I go," Lisa said.

"You mean wherever Enrico goes?" Stevie asked.

"Oh, of course! How could I have missed that?" Lisa said, realizing that Veronica found something very attractive about Enrico—his father's bank account. "She's really pathetic, isn't she?"

"Don't worry about this morning," Stevie said. "We'll see that she stays far away from you and Enrico. It's a promise."

Lisa knew that a promise from Stevie was like money in the bank, but she was curious to see what her friend had in mind.

Half an hour later, the girls had put on their walking shoes and packed everything else. They checked their bags at the hotel desk and waited for the Italian boys to pick them up for their morning jaunt. Mrs. Reg and Max were there, handing out street maps and checking watches.

"I don't know about this, Max. London is a big city," said Mrs. Reg. "Do you really think it's safe to let these youngsters out on their own?"

"Mother, let me remind you that we regularly allow them free rein with some of the most valuable things we own: our horses. If we can trust them with the likes of Topside and Prancer, don't you think we should trust them to go to a museum in broad daylight, just a couple of blocks from our hotel?"

Mrs. Reg frowned a little bit.

Max continued. "And if we don't let them go by themselves, we'll have to go with them . . ."

"I suppose you're right," said Mrs. Reg.

The Italian boys arrived then, along with their coach,

who seemed to be looking forward to some peaceful time with Max and Mrs. Reg. They were ready to go.

"Is *everyone* going to the museum?" Veronica asked. Although it was a general question, Veronica's eyes were on Enrico. That irritated Lisa. And it irritated her all the more because she knew Veronica knew the answer. She was about to say as much when Stevie came to her rescue.

"Oh, look, Lisa. Here, on the map. It's the place you wanted to get to—the London Dungeon. It's just cram-filled with really disgusting and gory stuff. They show people who are being tortured and even somebody who's been beheaded. There's a whole special room just about the London fire. And then there's an exhibit on the plague— all those bodies . . . Anyway, it's right here. You two should get going right away. We'll see you at one."

Lisa took Enrico by the hand and they headed out the door before he could protest. As soon as they had rounded the corner, Lisa felt free to laugh. Enrico looked at her suspiciously.

"Torture? Plague? The London fire? Do we have to?" he asked. "I mean, if that's what *you* want . . ."

"Not at all, Enrico. I want to walk around, just as we planned. Stevie just saved us from having Veronica along."

Then Enrico understood. "You do have very good friends, don't you?"

"The best," she assured him.

They set out toward the nearest park, Kensington, by

40

themselves and free of Veronica. They passed Kensington Palace, where some of the royals lived. Lisa mused that it was hard to imagine living in a palace.

"Drafty, actually, I think," Enrico said. She realized with a start that Enrico's house was a lot like that!

Together they walked through the park and then out into the streets. They paid little attention to their route, only vaguely aware of the buildings they passed. They were lost in conversation.

"I wonder what Cummington Castle is going to be like," Lisa said. "Do you know anything about it?"

"I've seen pictures, if that's what you mean. It's large—really looks like a castle. There are high walls. There may even be a lake around it—"

"A moat?" Lisa supplied.

"Is that the word, 'moat'?" Enrico asked. Lisa nodded. "Well, yes, I think so. The last person to live in it was the Duke of Cummington, but I think he died in the Civil War."

"Like between the North and the South?" Lisa said.

Enrico looked at her for a second, and then he laughed. "Don't you Americans ever learn *any* history besides your own?" he asked.

"Oh, *that* Civil War," Lisa said. "The one with Oliver Cromwell?"

"That's the one," said Enrico. "If I remember correctly, the Parliamentarians, mostly Puritans like the ones who first settled in Plymouth, wanted to get rid of the king,

Charles the First, I think. But I don't remember much more than that."

Lisa was a good student and a curious one. When somebody said "Civil War," the first thing she thought about was the American Civil War, but she also knew something about English and European history.

"I remember now. The Puritans who opposed Charles were called Roundheads—something about the way they wore their hair. And the Royalists were called Cavaliers. Didn't you learn that in *your* history class?"

"I did, I'm sure," Enrico said. "You remembered better than I did."

"Well, I'd like to learn more about the duke before we get to Cummington Castle. I wish there were a library or something—"

She stopped. So did Enrico. There, right in front of them, stood a large building with a sign out front proclaiming it to be a library.

"Shall we?" she asked.

"Why not?" he answered. "It seems like fate!"

A few minutes later, they were seated at a long table with a small selection of books that a librarian had provided for them.

"You look up 'Cummington, Duke of,' " Lisa said. "I'll read about the Civil War."

In the next hour they learned a lot. They learned that the war had taken place some 350 years earlier, from 1642 to 1651. They focused on the early part when the Roundheads took over most of the land of Britain. The Royalists were terrified of them. Many wealthy ones, like Cummington, had tried to elude the invading forces with trickery, such as hiding their wealth. For the most part, they were not successful.

"Here's something about Cummington," Enrico said. "There's a whole chapter on the construction of the castle. Then it says that Cummington was a Cavalier, though he didn't fight personally. He sent many of his servants to do that for him. Apparently he was extremely wealthy and there's something here in a—what do you call this?"

"A footnote?"

"Yes, a footnote, something about how after he died, nobody ever found his wealth."

"Then I wonder how they knew he was wealthy?"

"The big castle, I guess. Anyway, there's a lot more information here—"

"Oh, but no time!" Lisa said, looking at her watch. It was 12:45.

"We'll learn more when we get there, I'm sure."

"Right," Lisa said, closing the book she'd been reading. She and Enrico took the volumes back to the librarian and thanked her. She smiled politely at them.

Then they *ran*. They had no time to walk back to the hotel. They were behind schedule, and Max would be furious if they kept him waiting.

Just when Lisa thought she couldn't run anymore, she

43

spotted a taxi. The driver took them back to the hotel. They arrived at 12:59.

"Where have you been?" Veronica asked as she dropped a booklet marked "London Dungeon" in a trash bin. Lisa looked at her with disbelief. Veronica had actually gone to the London Dungeon, expecting to find Enrico there!

"We went to a library," Enrico said.

Veronica looked at Lisa in disbelief.

"Ah, the bus is here," said Max. "Everybody bring your bags out. It's time to be on our way. The *real* trip is just beginning."

6

"LOOK, THERE IT is!" Lisa cried excitedly, looking out the window at Cummington Castle.

"Turrets!" Stevie declared.

"Banners!" said Carole.

"Tents for the show horse stalls!" said Max.

"A moat!" said Enrico. His friends looked at him in surprise. He translated the word into Italian for them. They nodded.

Cummington Castle looked like a fairy-tale castle. It stood on a rise, silhouetted against the blue sky of the English countryside. It had a huge wall surrounding the castle, with crenellations on the battlements.

"Can you imagine villagers and soldiers pouring boiling oil on attacking hordes?" Stevie asked.

They could.

"And the best part about it is that the castle has been modernized," Max said. "It's got heat, electricity, and plumbing. Parts of it are used as a hotel, sort of a very posh bed-and-breakfast."

"Is that where we're staying?" Veronica asked.

"Not exactly," Max explained. "We're at the Steede Inn. I thought that sounded like a good place for us and my travel agent recommended it."

Veronica smiled tolerantly. "How quaint," she said.

The bus pulled up to the Steede. As far as The Saddle Club was concerned, it was great. For one thing, it *was* quaint. It had small rooms filled with comfortable furniture, curtains and pillows were carefully matched. It was both warm and homey. They entered the hotel lobby and peered into the pub that shared the ground floor with the dining room.

The Italian boys were staying in the inn's annex, across a courtyard. The Horse Wise team was in the main building. A bellman picked up Mrs. Reg's suitcase and led the group to their rooms. As they followed, they could tell that the Steede was a very old hotel and had been added onto many times. They made endless turns, then went up one step, around a corner, through a public room, down two steps, up a staircase.

"We'll never find our way out," Veronica complained.

"That's fine by me," said Stevie, looking at the comfortable furniture and pretty windows. "I'd be glad to move in."

"Just a few steps more, miss," said the bellman. And it was. He produced a key and opened a door into a large, airy room that had two twin beds and a fold-out cot.

"That's us," declared Carole, leading the way in. She, Stevie, and Lisa were sharing a room. It was bright and welcoming. The three girls piled in and closed the door. They heard the bellman deliver Mrs. Reg to the room next to theirs. Max's room was across the hall. Next to his was Veronica's room. The Saddle Club heard a brief silence after the bellman opened the door to her room.

"There's been some mistake," said Veronica. "This isn't a room. This is a closet."

"No mistake, miss," the bellman said politely. "It's the last single room available in the hotel."

The door shut firmly. The Saddle Club giggled to themselves. Nothing seemed to be working out for Veronica and while they weren't exactly worried about hurting her feelings, there didn't seem to be much point in rubbing it in by having her hear them laugh too loudly.

"Come on, let's get over to the castle," said Stevie. "It's just a short walk from here. We can be there in two minutes."

"You mean two minutes *after* we unpack, don't you?" Lisa asked.

Stevie gave her a look.

"Of course that's what she means," Carole said, answering for their friend. "Because as we unpack, we can take out our riding clothes, so that we can go to the stables and see if our horses have arrived and if they'd like a little exercise."

"Just what I had in mind," Stevie agreed.

It didn't take long. The girls hung up a few things, divided the drawer space, and had everything stowed in a matter of minutes. Five more minutes to put on their riding clothes and they were ready.

They checked in with Max, who said he'd meet them at the stables later, and they invited Veronica to come with them.

She glared and told them she was going to take a nap instead. The Saddle Club didn't mind at all. They headed off on their own.

The town of Cummington was quite small, and it only took the girls a few minutes to get to the castle. Up close, it was even more dramatic and wonderful than it had seemed as they'd driven past it. The walls surrounding the castle seemed to rise straight into the air. It was hard to imagine even trying to attack it.

The entrance to the castle was across a drawbridge that spanned the moat. Suspended above the main entrance was a portcullis, a spiked gate that could be lowered to keep out unwelcome visitors. Fortunately, The Saddle Club was welcome, and so, it seemed, were hundreds of other visitors.

Crowds of people milled about the castle and its

grounds. Since the actual show wasn't to begin until the next day, the girls figured that most of the visitors were there just to see the castle or to buy tickets for the show.

"I can't wait to see the place," said Stevie, leading her friends toward the drawbridge.

"Later," said Carole. "Our first concern is our horses. We've got to get to the stable to see if they've arrived from Dickens and to find out what we can be doing for them."

"And if we can ride them now, you mean," said Lisa.

"Definitely," said Carole.

"Good idea," Stevie agreed. She gave the stone turrets a final wave. "See you later," she promised. Then she followed her friends around the huge, imposing wall that protected Cummington.

The castle itself was on a hill, but the hill was smooth and grassy, dotted with only a few trees.

"I guess it's open so that the soldiers could see if anyone was attacking long before they got here," Stevie said.

"Maybe," said Lisa. "But that's assuming that this is the way it looked three hundred and fifty years ago. Remember, a lot of trees can grow and be cut down in that length of time. The castle certainly hasn't changed much—"

"Other than electricity, heating, and plumbing, you mean?"

"Well, yes, but I mean, the way it *looks*. The land around here, though. It could have been very different."

"For instance, there's no stable," said Carole, looking

around. "I'm sure there was one originally. A big castle like this would have had hundreds of horses to keep for all the soldiers—to say nothing of the duke himself. It probably wouldn't have fit inside the castle."

"Ah, but there's a stable now," said Stevie, pointing. And there, in front of them, was a huge expanse of tent, covering temporary stables where all the horses competing in the show would be housed.

"There must be room there for more than a hundred horses!" Lisa said, awed by the enormous expanse of striped canvas.

"It's not so surprising when you think about it," said Carole. "There are lots of competitors, and then there are the special-events horses, like ours. Remember, there are at least sixteen horses just for our demonstrations!"

"Oh, right," said Lisa. She was used to being the logical member of the group and she should have figured that out, but when it came to horses, sometimes Carole was more logical. "Let's go look," Lisa said.

The stable covered a large area, almost the size of a football field. There was a main entrance near the castle. The far entrance was more for horses, since it led to the arenas where competition would take place. There were three arenas. One was for the principal event, and it had stands and bleachers for an audience. The other two were for practice and warm-up.

The girls entered the temporary stable at the main entrance. They found a stable manager controlling entrances and exits.

"We're from America," Lisa began to explain.

"I can see that," grumbled the old man. "But it don't mean you're welcome to visit the horses."

"I mean, we're here as competitors. We're the American Pony Club team."

"Why didn't you say so?" he grumbled.

"I tried to," she said.

"The 'orses from Dickens arrived this morning." Then he riffled through a stack of papers clipped onto a board. "Aisle two, stalls fifteen to eighteen. That way," he pointed. He handed them each a sheet of paper with instructions for competitors and demonstrators and sent them on their way.

Before they could get to their own horses, they found someone they wanted to see even more.

"Look! It's Nigel!" said Stevie, quickening her pace. The others hurried, too. At aisle 1, stall 12, Nigel Hawthorne was checking the grooming job on a huge gray stallion.

"Well, if it isn't The Saddle Club!" Nigel said, greeting them all with a warm hug.

"We just got here," Stevie explained. "We were in London seeing absolutely everything we could cram into three days, but now it's time to get down to business. That means horses. Can we meet yours?"

"You certainly may," said Nigel. "Ladies, I'd like to introduce you to Pound Sterling." He stepped away from the stall opening so they could see the horse in question. "Sterling—that's what I call him—is a Thoroughbred stallion, eight years old. He's a silvery gray, which is how he got his name, and he's the property of Lord Yaxley."

"Yaxley?" Lisa asked. "That's not what Max said. Are you sure you've got the right guy?"

Nigel laughed. "Absolutely," he assured them. "However, Max may have been uncertain about how to pronounce it. It *is* pronounced Yaxley, but it's spelled Y-A-W-E-L-K-E-S-L-E-I-G-H. We British have become expert at eliminating unnecessary vowels when we speak."

"Right, like Harcourt-St. Claire's-in-the-Wold becoming Hart-Sinclair," said Lisa.

"Oh, that's right," said Nigel. "I heard a rumor that you were all riding horses from Dickens. It's true, then?"

"Yes, it is, and I guess we're going to have to do a super job to live up to Dickens's reputation."

"You'll do your best and that's all anybody expects," Nigel said. The girls knew that was true. It was just that they expected their best to earn first place.

"And what about you?" Lisa asked, admiring the sleek stallion in the stall. "Is Sterling as wonderful as he looks?"

"I think so," said Nigel. "Lord Yaxley doesn't seem convinced, though. He's been grumbling for months that this fellow isn't worth what he paid for him and he'll never get his money out in stud fees, either. He's been hoping for a big win to increase the horse's value so he can sell Sterling at a huge profit. I'd like to oblige him, and I'm sure Sterling has the skills and the power. Besides, it would be good for me to ride one of Yaxley's horses to a blue ribbon."

Carole looked at Sterling. It was hard for her to imagine a horse like that disappointing anyone. "Don't worry," she assured Nigel. "You'll do well on him."

"With the proper cheering section," he said.

"We'll be there for you," said Stevie. "And we'll make all the noise we can muster."

"Which is quite a lot," Lisa said.

"I'll be listening for it," said Nigel. Then he glanced at his watch. "Right now, however, I've got to get to a team meeting. See you three tomorrow!"

He gave Sterling a final pat and left the girls to find their way to aisle 2, stalls 15 to 18. It didn't take long. There, waiting patiently for them, were Miss Havisham, Copperfield, Pip, and Nickleby. They looked well adjusted to their new surroundings. Carole explained to her friends that that probably meant they were used to being transported and spending time in unfamiliar stables.

"In other words, I think they compete a lot," said Carole.

"I think we're very lucky to have these horses to ride," said Lisa.

"It's not luck, it's you," said Stevie. "Just because you rescued Tessa when she'd been thrown by her horse the last time you were in England . . ."

Lisa shrugged. "I was just doing what every good rider does when another gets into trouble. I was being helpful. And now she's being helpful back."

"I like her kind of helpful," Stevie said, giving Copperfield a hug. He nuzzled her neck and tickled her, making her laugh.

Pip stuck his head out over the stall door and looked around, peering first one way down the aisle and then the other.

"I guess he's curious," said Lisa, patting him affectionately.

"I think he's just looking for the door," said Carole. "These horses have spent as much time in the van as we did in the bus. I bet they'd like to get out."

"Like to go for a ride?" Stevie asked. She thought she knew what was on Carole's mind, and she liked it.

"Yes, but how do we do it?" Carole asked.

Lisa knew the answer. She held up the sheet of paper that the stable manager had handed her. "We apply at the lads' booth for someone to tack up our mounts," she read.

"What?" asked Stevie.

"It means we go ask a stable boy to do our jobs for us," Lisa explained.

"I can live with that," said Stevie.

Half an hour later, three stablehands, known in England as lads, even though one of them was a woman, led their horses to one of the schooling rings and held the reins as the girls mounted.

At first the girls just walked their horses around the schooling ring. It gave the horses a chance to limber up. It gave the girls a chance to talk about what they wanted to accomplish in their practice ride.

"We have to do well in our competition," Carole said.

"I thought that was what I was supposed to say," Stevie joked.

"I don't mean we have to win, although I wouldn't mind that. What I did mean is that we are sort of ambassadors for Pony Clubs and we want to be sure we represent the organization well," Carole explained.

"That won't be any problem at all as long as I'm riding a wonderful horse like Copperfield," said Stevie. "He's just about perfect—almost as good as Belle." Stevie loved her own horse, Belle, better than any other horse anywhere, but that didn't mean she couldn't enjoy riding Copperfield when Belle wasn't around.

Carole nudged Miss Havisham into a trot. The horse picked up the gait immediately, flicking her tail proudly. "This one's a lot of fun, too," said Carole.

Copperfield trotted on after Miss Havisham. Next Lisa nudged Pip. He remained at a walk. That was unusual. Most of the time when a horse in front of another changed gaits, the horse behind automatically took it up. Lisa nudged again, but Pip stubbornly refused to go faster. This wasn't at all like the behavior Pip had shown just two days earlier at Tessa's house. Lisa was surprised, but realized that perhaps it was because he was more upset by the long trip than the others.

"Come on, Lisa," Carole said. "Get him moving!"

Lisa nudged Pip again, this time harder, almost a kick. She also jangled the reins a bit. It wasn't great riding form, but it might get Pip's attention. It did. He started cantering and zipped by the others. This was downright naughty behavior on Pip's part, and Lisa couldn't let him get away with it. She tightened up on the reins to bring him back to a trot. He shook his head rebelliously and then stopped.

This was not a good sign.

"I'm doing something wrong," Lisa said.

"Don't be silly," Carole said, drawing up next to her. She reached over and patted Pip on the neck reassuringly. "I think he's just being fussy because he's in a strange place. Once he gets down to some serious riding, he'll forget all about his surroundings and only pay attention to you. Let's start again at a walk."

Lisa nudged him and Pip began walking. The next time Carole started trotting on Miss Havisham, Pip trotted, too, but it wasn't an easy gait as it had been the other day. Although he obliged Lisa and followed her directions, he didn't seem a willing participant. After half an hour of riding, she'd had enough.

"Maybe he just needs to rest a little bit more," she said.

"Maybe," Stevie agreed. "And maybe we should do the same. Max said that all of the Pony Club teams were going to have a dinner together tonight. We're going to have to shower and change first, so why don't we pack it in for the day and get back to the hotel?" Carole and Lisa agreed.

Riding when there were stablehands—lads—to do all the work was very different from riding at Pine Hollow, where the girls were responsible for their own horses.

"I think I could get used to this," said Stevie a few minutes later when the lad who was looking after Copperfield approached to help her out of the saddle.

Carole shook her head. "Not me," she said. "Riding is a lot more than climbing into the saddle, riding, and then climbing back out. It's about being totally responsible for your horse and knowing everything there is to know about his—uh, excuse me Miss Havisham, *her*—welfare. That's one thing Max is one hundred percent right about."

"But while we're here, can we just pretend it's okay to let someone else do the work?" Stevie asked.

"Okay." Carole relented, handing her reins to the lad waiting for her.

The three girls dismounted, thanked the lads, and left the stable to return to the hotel.

They were rounding the castle wall where the road led to the main street of Cummington town when they first saw Veronica.

"I thought she was taking a nap," said Carole.

"Why is it we always forget to never believe a word she says?" Stevie remarked.

57

"What is she doing?" asked Lisa. That was a better question than Stevie's because whatever Veronica was doing, it certainly looked strange.

The Saddle Club ducked behind a tree so they could watch Veronica without being readily visible. Veronica was walking around the grass outside of the castle wall, studying the area intensely. She looked around at the ground, and she looked around at the sky. Her eyes followed the bed of the creek that fed the castle's moat. There was a large old tree near where she stood. She studied it as well.

"She's flipped," said Stevie finally.

"Why do you say that?" asked Lisa. "She seems to know exactly what she's doing."

"Maybe these are the symptoms of severe shopping withdrawal," Stevie reasoned. "After all, she never did get to Harrods. So maybe she's just looking to see if there's a branch of Laura Ashley at the castle wall."

Lisa didn't think it was a very likely explanation, but it was as good as any.

"Maybe," she conceded.

"And maybe we don't have to pay any attention to her," said Carole. "Let's get back to the hotel."

They cut across the grass to the road to return to the hotel. Whatever Veronica was doing, she was concentrating too intensely to notice them, and that was all right as far as The Saddle Club was concerned.

SIXTEEN PONY CLUBBERS and all four of their coaches, plus Mrs. Reg, met in the hotel lobby that night to go out to dinner.

"I'm Miss Thimbleby," said the English coach. "Everybody calls me Thim, though, so you might as well, too." The Pony Clubbers and their coaches spent the next few minutes exchanging names. It was easy for the Horse Wise group and the Italian boys, because they knew one another. The English riders and the Dutch took a little longer to remember. Also, the Dutch coach had a very long name—Herr von Heudenbroek. Lisa hoped she'd never have to call him anything!

Thim continued. "Since you're here in our nation, we

think of ourselves as your hosts, and so we are inviting you all out to dinner tonight. We've reserved a room upstairs at one of the downtown restaurants—"

"There *is* a downtown here?" Veronica whispered to Lisa. "All I saw was a little village."

"—of course, downtown is just the little village of Cummington," Thim went on. "So it will only take us a few minutes to walk there. Follow us, then. We've chosen a place called Azzip. It's famous for having the best pizza within a twenty-kilometer radius of Cummington. Isn't that just mouthwatering? We thought that would be a special treat for you young visitors."

The news was more than a little surprising to the American girls. The Saddle Club was beginning to think that the only food available in England was pizza.

"Have you ever heard of the idea of too much of a good thing?" Stevie asked her friends.

"Oh, don't make such a fuss," said Lisa. "Everybody is just trying to be nice to us."

"Maybe they'll be a little less nice to us tomorrow so we can have hamburgers."

"Shhh," Carole hushed her. "We are guests, you know."

"I know," said Stevie. "Besides, I really do love pizza. I think I do. At least, I used to."

Lisa stifled a giggle. Stevie was being funny, but nobody wanted to hurt anybody's feelings.

"*Avanti*," said the Italian boys. They began their brief walk downtown.

Lisa was pleased to find Enrico walking beside her.

"Did you have a good ride this afternoon?" he asked.

"I did and I didn't," Lisa said truthfully. "My horse—his name is Pip—was giving me trouble. I don't know why, either. The other day when I rode him, he was such a dream. Carole, Stevie, and I think that maybe he fussed because he's in a new place."

"Ah, perhaps," said Enrico. Lisa smiled to herself. She loved the way Enrico said "perhaps." Although he spoke excellent English with almost no accent, there were some words that just had a nice lilt to them. "Perhaps" was one of them. It came out more like "puh-heps."

"We'll just have to see how he behaves tomorrow," said Lisa. "I've got to say, though, if he's as naughty tomorrow as he was today, the American team will not be taking home any blue ribbons."

"Ah, perhaps you don't have to worry about that," said Enrico. "Since the Italian team will doubtlessly be performing at its best, it will not be your horse's fault that the team does not win." There was a twinkle in his eye. It was a challenge and Lisa intended to meet it.

"Puh-heps we'll see," she said.

"Hmmm," he responded. Then he took her arm and tucked it around his so that they could walk closer together. They didn't stay together long, however. Much to Lisa's surprise, she found herself being jostled away from Enrico, and, before she knew it, he had let go of her arm and Veronica was walking between them.

"Is the restaurant this way?" Veronica asked Enrico, talking only to him as if Lisa had disappeared from the face of the earth.

"Since the whole group appears to be walking in that direction, I would say that is correct," Enrico answered her. Lisa couldn't believe how polite he was being.

"Of course it is!" she snapped at Veronica.

Veronica didn't look at her.

"I just love pizza," said Veronica. "But I don't think the pizza in America or England is anywhere near as good as the pizza in your homeland, Enrico. Don't you agree?"

Enrico was about to answer her when Stevie's voice rose above the crowd.

"Oh, look at that jewelry store!" she said loudly, pointing across the narrow street. It was more than Veronica could resist. She excused herself from Enrico and scooted across the street just as the rest of the group was entering the restaurant.

It was a cozy restaurant, much like the pub in the inn where they were staying. The building was old, with dark brown beams crossing the ceiling. They followed the owner up a narrow set of stairs to what must have once been a loft and now served as a small room for private parties. Their tables were all laid out and waiting for them. The owner assured the riders that their pizza would be there in a few minutes.

By the time Veronica rejoined the group, complaining that the jewelry store had little more than costume jewelry to offer, Lisa and Enrico were seated at a table for eight with Stevie, two boys from Holland, and three of the English riders. There was no room for Veronica. Stevie winked at Lisa. Lisa smiled back. Stevie was a *very* good friend. But she'd always known that.

Veronica, however, was undaunted. She tapped one of the Dutch boys on his shoulder and told him that his friend wanted him to sit at the other table. The boy was so polite that he moved to the other table and was seated before he had time to wonder exactly who it was who had wanted him there. Once he'd moved, Veronica slid happily into his seat, directly across from Enrico.

In a few minutes the pizza was delivered. The buzz of conversation quieted while the young riders delved into the crusty, crisp pizza that was the specialty of the house. By the time everyone was reaching for a second slice, Thim stood up to speak.

"I have some good news for all of you," she began. "On the second night of the three-day event—that means not tomorrow night, but the night after—we are all invited to a ball at the castle."

"A ball! But I don't have anything to wear!" Veronica practically exploded. It was so typically Veronica that The Saddle Club almost laughed out loud.

"You don't need a ballgown for this," Thim said. "It's actually a costume ball. In honor of the Duke of Cummington, costume will be of the Civil War era. The Pony Clubbers from Skelton Green—that's my team, in case you don't know it—will be glad to help any of you put together your outfits. The dance itself isn't very formal, but a Civil War ball is always a fun event and this should be no exception!"

"Civil War? Why, I can go as Scarlett O'Hara!" Veronica declared. Then, as if it were a cue to herself, she fell into character, selecting Enrico as her hero. "Oooh, Rhett," she began in a phony Southern accent.

"Wrong Civil War," Lisa corrected her. "This is the English Civil War. The Puritans in Parliament, known as the Roundheads, opposed the king's men, the Cavaliers. Eventually they overthrew King Charles the First, and even beheaded him, leaving the country under the rule of Oliver Cromwell until Charles the Second returned to England to claim the throne after Cromwell's death. That was three hundred fifty years ago, in the sixteen-forties. The Duke of Cummington was a Cavalier, but he never actually fought. He remained in his castle, guarding it against occasional Roundhead raiders."

"How did you know all this?" Carole asked, impressed.

"I told you," Lisa said. "We went to the library this morning."

"You actually *meant* that?" Veronica blurted out.

"Of course," said Lisa. "Where did you think we were?"

Veronica ignored her question and countered with another one. "What else did you learn about this guy Cummington?"

"Not much," said Lisa. "We were just getting to that

64

part when we realized we had to get back to the hotel. I mean, we found out that he was pretty rich, but I guess we can tell that by the size of his house."

The other riders laughed at that.

Enrico continued the explanation, telling the last of what they'd learned. "There was a—what did you call it, footnote?—yes, footnote. Something about how nobody ever knew exactly how much wealth he had because it was never found."

"It probably got stolen," Lisa said. "A lot of that happened."

"Definitely," Veronica assured them. Her certainty surprised The Saddle Club. "I mean, in a war, a lot of people steal a lot of things. I'm sure that must be what happened. It only makes sense, doesn't it?"

Lisa thought it did make sense, but she also thought it rather odd that Veronica should be the one to have any common sense about a treasure. She shrugged it off. Veronica acting strange was nothing new. She had much more interesting things to think about, such as would her third slice of pizza be pepperoni or plain?

Enrico, however, was curious. He turned to one of the English riders, a young girl who'd been very quiet the whole time. Lisa remembered that her name was Ashley Hanna. "Do you know any more of the story of Lord Cummington?" Enrico asked.

Ashley seemed pleased to be asked. "Well, there *are* stories, of course, but one doesn't know whether to believe them or not. There are a great many tales from that era, most of them apocryphal," she said.

"A-poc-what?" asked Enrico.

"It means of doubtful authenticity," said Veronica, smiling at Enrico.

Lisa didn't care whether the tales were true or not. She thought it would be fun to hear some of the stories and was about to ask Ashley to tell one when Veronica broke into the conversation again.

"If we go as Cavaliers, we can wear fancy clothes, can't we?" she asked.

"Oh, yes!" said Ashley brightly. "The Cavaliers were the king's men and women. The Roundheads were the Puritans. The king's men wore very fancy clothes indeed. At the Civil War costume balls I've read about, only the very wealthy guests come as Cavaliers. They are the only ones who can afford to dress in that manner."

Veronica's face fell. "Oh, dear," she said. "All my good jewelry is back in the States. I had no idea when I was packing . . ."

People who didn't know Veronica were often surprised when she said things like that. All the other young riders seemed confused, but Veronica didn't surprise The Saddle Club at all. It delighted Stevie because it gave her the opportunity to let Veronica make even more of a fool of herself.

"Veronica, you know it's only midafternoon in Virginia

now. You still have time to call home and have the maid pack up a gown and some proper jewelry and send it here by express service. It'll arrive in plenty of time for the ball."

Carole had an idea, too. "Or, you could go to the jewelry store across the street when it's open and buy a few bangles to dress up whatever you have here."

"You're right! I could," Veronica said excitedly. "It's really not too late, is it? Is there a phone here?"

"I'm sure I saw a pay telephone in the hallway downstairs," Ashley said.

"Excuse me, please," Veronica said, standing up. She went to the stairs and disappeared into the hallway.

"I thought she was joking," Ashley said. "But she seems serious about this. Is that right?"

"Dead serious," Stevie assured her.

"Oh, dear. I never should have told her about the costumes. It'll be such a bother for her and it doesn't have to be. The costumes are all for fun, you know."

"Dressing is never just fun for Veronica," Stevie said. "Besides, it wasn't your fault."

"No, I guess some things can't be helped," Ashley said.

"Veronica definitely falls into that category," Stevie assured her. "She can't be helped." Ashley smiled at Stevie's joke and then offered her another slice of pizza. When everybody had had another slice, the talk turned to horses—a common topic for everyone in the room.

Lisa thought it was wonderful to be with so many other people who shared her love of horses. It was a Pony Club event, but it almost felt like an international Saddle Club meeting, too. Everybody seemed to want to help everybody else. When Lisa mentioned that her horse had been giving her a hard time that afternoon, Ashley suggested that perhaps it was just a matter of the new stall.

"My horse always takes a day to adjust. I'm sure Pip will be fine tomorrow."

"Sometimes it isn't just a new place," Henrik, one of the Dutch boys, said. "The water or the grain is different from home and that upsets a fussy horse. I bet that's it. Again, he'll adjust in a day or so, but, of course, not in time to save Horse Wise from the terrible defeat it will suffer at the hands of the Netherlands team."

There was a sparkle in Stevie's eyes. "Don't count on it," she said to Henrik. "Based on past experience, Horse Wise would beat your team if one of our horses were on crutches!"

"Haven't you people ever heard of 'home field advantage'?" Ashley asked brightly. Everybody laughed.

While the others continued their talk about horses in general, Enrico was concerned with Pip.

"Do you think perhaps he might be ill?" he asked.

"I didn't see any signs of that," Lisa said. "But I don't know him well."

"Maybe you should check on him tonight," Enrico said.

Lisa thought that was a good idea and told him so. "I'm going to ask Max if I can go over there now."

"And I will come along. Would that be all right? Or would you think I'm trying to sabotage Pip so that my team can win?" he asked, teasing her.

"I think it would, perhaps, be all right," she said.

In a few minutes, she'd gotten permission from Max. He told her to be back at the hotel by nine-thirty. Enrico looked at his watch and nodded solemnly.

"I promise," he said.

Lisa told Stevie and Carole where she was going.

"Check Pip's feed," Carole said.

"And his hooves. Maybe he's picked up a stone."

"Take his pulse," Henrik said. "And his temperature— there's a medical kit next to my horse's stall if you need it. It has a stethoscope in it."

"Thanks," Lisa said. She hoped she wouldn't need those things, but she was grateful for the offer.

"And if there's a problem, our team has an extra horse you could ride," said Ashley.

"He's a good mount, too," Thim added.

"Thank you," Lisa repeated. "I appreciate it. I'll let you all know what we find. Good night!"

With that, they went downstairs. Veronica was just hanging up the phone when they reached the hallway.

"Can you believe it? I can't get through," she said to Enrico, practically gushing to him. Then she turned to

Lisa. "Say, did you notice if there's a fax machine at our hotel?" she asked.

Veronica *was* desperate, but Lisa couldn't help her. "No, I didn't," Lisa said. "But I'm sure if there is you'll find it," she added.

"You bet I will," Veronica assured her.

A BRIGHT SUMMER moon seemed to sparkle through the tree branches, casting long shadows on the streets of Cummington. It was a cool night. Enrico took Lisa's hand and they walked together to the tented stables at the castle.

"I don't think I understand your friend, Veronica," Enrico said.

Lisa wasn't inclined to be generous toward Veronica, but the image of her practically throwing herself at Enrico on the way out of the restaurant was more pathetic than annoying. Veronica was obviously jealous of Lisa, and that was so outrageous that it brought out some sympathy in Lisa. "I'm not sure anyone understands her," Lisa said kindly. "She can be very difficult to be around, but sometimes there are moments when she's almost normal. And then, just when you get to like her, she does something laughable, like having her maid send her an evening dress and jewelry."

"I think she will look quite lovely," Enrico said.

"Count on it," Lisa assured him. "She wears nothing but the best. But it's not her clothes that are really important to anyone but her."

"What, then?" Enrico asked.

"She's a good rider. She's been doing it for a long time. She's had a lot of lessons and, in spite of herself, she's learned. She'll do well for the team."

"Then that is what counts," Enrico said. "Horses, always horses." He squeezed her hand affectionately.

"You've got that right," Lisa said, squeezing back. It was nice to be walking through a picturesque village with a handsome boy. One of the nicest parts was knowing that they shared an interest in horses. Something glinted in the moonlight from the sidewalk and caught Lisa's eye. She stopped and looked. Then she reached down for the shiny object.

"What's that?" Enrico asked.

"I think it's a button," said Lisa. She picked it up. It was, in fact, a button with a rhinestone stud in it.

"Imagine how annoyed your friend Veronica would be if it were her button."

"Oh, she'd never wear something as plain as a rhinestone!" Lisa teased. "For her, it would have to be a real diamond button!"

Enrico laughed. Lisa dropped the button in her pocket, thinking, as she did, about the difference between fakes and the real thing. Veronica would consider herself the real thing, but her teammates knew she was a fake.

"I think we turn here to go to the castle," Enrico said. It was a welcome interruption to her thoughts. They left the streets and began the pleasant walk along the long road that led to the castle grounds. It was an open area. There were few trees and no people. They walked in contented silence. The road circled the castle's wall and then split, one way leading into the castle, the other toward the stabling area.

There was a large old oak tree not far from the stables on the banks of the small creek that fed into the castle's moat. Lisa remembered the tree from this afternoon. In the daytime, it had offered a haven of shade from the bright sunlight. Its huge trunk suggested that it had been there a very long time, perhaps several hundred years.

"Do you think that oak was there when the duke lived here?" Lisa asked as she and Enrico crossed the wooden bridge over the creek.

"Perhaps as a tiny seed, what do you call it?"

"Acorn."

"Yes, acorn," Enrico said. "I don't think that any tree, really, lives that long."

Lisa made a note to tell him about the giant redwoods

of California, but later, because right then, the tree's shadow moved, startling both Lisa and Enrico.

"What was that?" Lisa asked.

The shadow moved again before Enrico could answer, and then they both knew it wasn't a shadow; it was a man. He was standing under the oak tree, looking around as if to get his bearings.

"Can we help you?" Enrico offered as they approached the man.

"No thanks," he said, tugging at his cap. "Just having a walk of a summer's eve."

Lisa and Enrico nodded to the man, who hurried off, limping, back down the road that had brought them to the stable. His uneven stride could be heard along the road behind them as they entered the stable. It made Lisa remember their original reason for coming tonight. She hoped Pip's problem wasn't any kind of lameness.

The two of them stepped into the cover of the dark stables and stopped, waiting for their eyes to become accustomed to the dimness. The place was filled with the wonderful sounds and smells of horses. To the right, a horse stomped impatiently on the ground. Ahead, another munched lazily on some hay. One snorted softly. Another answered with a gentle whinny.

"Isn't it wonderful?" Lisa whispered to Enrico. "All these great horses in one place?"

"It ain't nuffin' compared to what used to be 'ere, you know," said a gruff voice from the darkness.

"What?" Lisa said.

"Where are you?" Enrico asked.

"Roight over 'ere," said the voice.

A small desk lamp snapped on, and just to their left, at the desk, was an old man, perhaps seventy.

"Name's 'Ank," he said. "Oi'm the lad what looks after the 'orses at night."

Lisa translated quickly in her mind. This was a man named Hank who was the night watchman among the stablehands—the "lads."

The old man stood up and offered his hand. Lisa and Enrico shook it and introduced themselves.

"Oi know 'oo you are," he said. It turned out that he'd seen both of them riding that afternoon. "Even when Oi'm not on duty, there isn't much Oi don't know around 'ere," he said. "You two are part of them Pony Clubbers, roight?"

"Right," Lisa said. "And I'm riding one of the horses from Dickens," said Lisa.

"Fine 'orses," 'Ank said.

"Oh, yes," said Lisa. "We came over to check on Pip, though. I was riding him this afternoon and he was fussy as can be. When I rode him the other day at Dickens, he didn't show a bit of that fussiness. I hope he's okay."

"Well, then let's take a look at 'im," 'Ank said. He picked up a flashlight and led the two young riders along the aisle to Pip's stall. Lisa was very aware of the fact that even though there were more than fifty horses stabled at

Cummington, 'Ank didn't even have to consult a chart. He knew just where to find Pip.

When they got to the stall, 'Ank flipped a switch to light up the area.

Pip was there. He looked just fine. His ears perked curiously toward his visitors. His eyes were bright and welcoming. Lisa held out a hand. Pip came over for a pat. She obliged him happily.

'Ank slipped into the stall. He ran his hands over the horse expertly. He lifted each hoof and checked the feet for tenderness. There was no swelling on the legs. His feed bucket was empty, as it should be, and his hay and water showed that he'd been eating and drinking just the way any healthy horse would.

"Nothin' wrong 'ere that I can see," 'Ank said.

"What about his mouth?" Lisa asked. "He seemed to flinch every time I moved the reins."

'Ank checked Pip's mouth, but there were no sores that might explain his behavior. "But if he gave you trouble when you moved the reins, maybe we'd better look at his tack," said 'Ank.

Enrico and Lisa followed him over to the tack area for the Dickens horses, and there they found the answer. There was a chart identifying the tack for each of the horses, and at Pip's name it called for the bridle identified as "P"—presumably for Pip. The bridle hung on the hook marked with Pip's name was "J." It was a double bridle with a curb bit. The "P" bridle, hung on another hook

76

away from the rest of the tack, was a single bridle with a plain broken snaffle bit. A curb bit was tough on a horse's mouth. A broken snaffle was a gentle bit, the right choice for a horse with a soft mouth that responded quickly to a gentle signal.

"That's the answer, then," Lisa said. "The lad made a mistake when he tacked up Pip."

" 'E shouldn't 'ave made a mistake like that!" 'Ank grumbled. "These lads today . . ."

Lisa didn't think there was much point in grumbling about the lads of today. The fact was that she was used to tacking up her own horse and if she had done it—as Max would have wanted her to—this wouldn't have happened.

Lisa knew there was nothing wrong with a curb bit. They were absolutely appropriate for many horses. But they were much harsher than a snaffle, and if a horse was used to a snaffle, the sudden change to a curb bit would make him flinch.

"It's okay, 'Ank," she said, reassuring the old man. "Now we know what was wrong. There's no damage to Pip's mouth and I'll be sure he's got the right tack on tomorrow." She took the "J" bridle and set it off to the side. The "P" bridle was hung where it belonged.

"Aye, Miss Lisa," he said. "That you will, I'm sure of it." He and Lisa each gave Pip a final good-night pat and they turned out the light at the stall. Then 'Ank led the way back to his desk.

"Every horse is different from every other," 'Ank said,

almost talking to himself. "It's a mistake for a lad, or a lass, not to know that. The ones that do know their horses, now they are the ones that become fine riders."

Lisa knew that was a compliment. It made her blush and she was glad that neither 'Ank nor Enrico could see that in the dark stable.

"Fine riders, I mean, like the old duke 'imself."

"How would you know that?" Enrico asked.

"Father to son," 'Ank said. "Father to son."

"You mean your father—" Lisa began, but then she stopped herself. "No, the duke died more than three hundred years ago!"

"And it was my great, great, oh, Oi don't know 'ow many 'greats' there should be there, but in my family, we call them all Gran. Still, it's my Gran's been lookin' after the 'orses at Cummington since the time o' William the Conqueror. And every father tells every son everything he knows."

"You know about the duke?" Lisa asked. "The last one, I mean?"

"Aye, Miss Lisa, that I do," he said. He settled back into his chair and nodded toward a nearby bench where Lisa and Enrico could sit.

A warm, familiar feeling swept over Lisa. It took her a second to identify it; then she knew. 'Ank was about to tell her and Enrico a story. It felt just like the times Mrs. Reg told stories to the riders at Pine Hollow. The only difference was that Mrs. Reg couldn't stand to see idle hands, so they were usually cleaning tack when she talked. Lisa settled onto the bench with Enrico, and the two of them listened.

"'E was a mean, stingy old man, that last Duke of Cummington. It weren't always so. When he was young, he'd had two great loves. The first was the fair Lady Elizabeth. He adored her when they were wee children. He wed her when they were of age. He told my Gran once that she was the sun in his day. He couldn't do enough for her. He bought her jewels, diamonds, pearls from the Orient, rubies, opals, you name it, Lady Elizabeth got it from 'is Lordship. His other great love was 'orses—one in particular. He had a stallion—pure silvery white he was— looked a lot like that fellow Sterling that your friend is riding, Miss Lisa. The duke adored 'is stallion almost as much as he adored 'is missus. He built a whole stable just for the horse. Wasn't anybody but the duke could ride him, either. That man was the only one the horse would let on his back. If anybody else tried to do so much as take him out of the stall, he'd rear and stomp and he wouldn't stop until the interloper had run off or was dead. But he'd hold still for the duke. The man could *talk* to the horse.

"Then one day, Lady Elizabeth disappeared. Nobody ever knew exactly what happened except that Gran said she run off with one of them Roundhead fellows, but I don't know. A lady like that, all them jewels . . ."

"Didn't she take them with her?"

"Not a bit. Left every one behind," said 'Ank. "It was like she done it to spite the duke, like she was saying *his* jewels weren't good enough for her."

'Ank shook his head as if he couldn't understand Lady Elizabeth's reasoning. Then he continued his story.

" 'E was a changed man after that. Never a smile, never a kind word to anyone. It was like he couldn't trust anybody ever again. The only being in the whole world that he trusted were his horse. And the horse come to be everything to him."

"Oh, dear," Enrico said. "No wonder he became bitter."

"Bitter is the right word. He become cruel, too. And 'eartless."

"Artless?" Enrico asked.

"Heartless," Lisa explained.

'Ank went on. "It was the Civil War then, you know. The Roundheads controlled a lot of the towns around here, but not Cummington. The duke hated them Roundheads, not because they opposed his king, but because one had stolen his bride. He would rather have died than give them the satisfaction of having so much as one pearl of Elizabeth's jewels. He took every single piece of jewelry he'd ever given her—the whole was worth a fortune—and he buried it all in the one place he knew it would be safe —the place no man but him dared venture."

"The stallion?" Lisa asked. 'Ank nodded solemnly.

"Right under the stallion's stall, mind you. No treasure was worth a man's life, and it would take a life to move the stallion. The duke 'ardly went out after that. He provided some of his own men to fight for the king, but he didn't really care what happened in the war, as long as his lands and treasure was safe from the 'ands of the Roundheads.

"And then, one night, there was a fire. Nobody knows how it started, not even Gran. The blaze swept through the stable, destroying the building and all that was in it—"

"The stallion?" Lisa asked.

"Aye, the stallion. He was gone. In the end, there weren't nothing but ashes left. They couldn't even find the remains of the horse to bury. There was no sign of the stable, the horse, or the treasure. The duke didn't talk of the treasure, though. He spoke only of his horse and he swore revenge on those who murdered the steed. He was convinced it was the rebel Roundheads, but nobody was ever punished for the fire. The duke spent the next twelve months stalking about his castle. He wouldn't leave the grounds, nor talk to a livin' soul.

"And then, exactly twelve months to the day after the mysterious fire, the duke was found dead. There's no explanation for his death. He wasn't sick; he didn't do anything to himself and there were no wounds. He was just dead. He was found, lyin' amid the foundations of the old stable. In his right hand, he clutched a single fire opal."

There was a long silence as Lisa and Enrico absorbed the amazing story.

"He'd been digging the treasure up?" Enrico finally asked.

"There weren't no signs of any digging," 'Ank said. "And there never 'ave been. To this day, nobody knows how the fire that killed the stallion started. Nobody knows how the duke died. And nobody knows what become of the treasure. Nothing but the fire opal 'as ever been seen of it."

"What 'appened to the castle?" Lisa asked. "I mean happened."

"Once the duke was dead them Round'eads took it for their own."

"And the treasure?" asked Lisa.

"Gran said it would be found someday."

"Really?" Lisa whispered.

"Yes," 'Ank said solemnly. "The duke told 'im, and 'e told 'is son and 'is son told *'is* son and so on down to me that the treasure will be found one day by a rider with foyre in his 'eart."

The old man's eyes sparkled in the dim light. It sent a chill of excitement through Lisa. It was a thrill and a promise—both at once.

"What a wonderful story!" Lisa said when she could speak.

Enrico nodded. Then he took her hand again. "I think it's time to get back to the hotel," he said.

It definitely was that. Lisa had to hurry. She couldn't wait to tell the story to Stevie and Lisa!

To: Mr. diAngelo, President Willow Creek Bank
From: Veronica diAngelo

Daddy,
  Sorry to bother you at the office, but it's important. They
are having a ball here day after tomorrow and I didn't bring
anything to wear. Can you believe they didn't tell us about
this until tonight? Please express my blue satin dress and the
shoes that match, plus appropriate accessories. Mother will
know what to send.
  There's something very exciting going on here. The
Chubbles told me about an old mystery and I think I have
an idea how to solve it! Can't wait to give you more news,

*but in the meantime, do you think you could get your hands
on a metal detector?*

Remember, it's the blue satin I want, not the silk.

Love,
Veronica

* * *

"'. . . AND THE TREASURE will only be found by a rider
with a foyre in 'is 'eart,'" Lisa said, finishing the story for
her friends.

"Foyre in 'is *art?*" Stevie asked.

"Fire in his *heart,*" Lisa said. "That's the way 'Ank says
things. It's an odd accent, but you'll get used to it. Wait
until you meet him!"

"How romantic!" Stevie said.

"That duke really loved his horse," Carole remarked.

"Definitely," Lisa agreed.

The three of them were in their pajamas in the room at
the inn. Max had already hushed them and told them to
go to sleep three times, but old 'Ank's story was too good
to wait until morning. Carole and Stevie loved it just as
much as Lisa had.

"It *is* a great story," said Carole. "But I wonder if people
actually believe it. I mean if there were a treasure, somebody would have found it in three hundred and fifty
years."

"That kind of story brings treasure-hunters for generations," said Stevie. "People are still tracking down supposed sunken galleons and pirate ships."

"And finding the treasures, too," Stevie said. "I know I read about one near Florida, I think it was. There were zillions of dollars' worth of treasure."

"Under the ocean is different from underground," Lisa said logically. "Enrico and I were looking at that big old oak tree—remember it?—and trying to figure out if it was there when the duke was alive. I thought it was possible, but he didn't agree. The only thing we can be sure of is that the stones of the castle are the same."

"How could anybody even know for sure where the stallion's stable was? It burned to the ground, remember? All we know is that it was outside of the castle. Lisa's right. Nothing's the same."

"Water would be the same," Stevie said. "Where there was a river three hundred and fifty years ago, there would probably be a river now."

"Or a stream," Lisa said.

"And any stable would have to have a water source," said Stevie. There was a look in her eye that indicated she was definitely getting an idea.

"Oh, stop it," Carole said. "Believe me, those jewels are long gone."

"I bet she's right," said Lisa. "Remember, the Round-heads took over the castle after the duke died. If they'd found the jewels, they would have just taken them. They wouldn't have made any great announcement. Either they never were there—like what if Lady Elizabeth actually took them herself?—or they were found by someone else."

"But who could keep the secret?" Stevie asked. She began talking more quickly—just the way she always did when she got one of her harebrained ideas. "All we have to do is to dig a little bit. They can't be all that deep. Or maybe they can . . . do you remember seeing a hardware store in town? We could probably pick up some shovels, maybe a metal detector—"

"*Stevie!*" Lisa said exasperatedly. "I think you're missing the point. The story is just that—a story. It doesn't matter if it's true or not because the jewels aren't what's important."

"They're important to me," Stevie protested.

"I bet they'd be important to Veronica, too," said Carole.

That made them all stop and think. Of course, Veronica would learn about a story like that. And, of course, she'd believe it. Most important, she'd think she was the one who was supposed to unearth the missing gems.

"That's why the little sneak was walking around the grounds!" Stevie hissed. "Why, if she thinks she can beat us to the treasure—"

"Stevie! Or should I say *Veronica*," Lisa said pointedly.

"Am I that bad?" Stevie asked.

"Only sometimes," Lisa said, calming her friend. "But don't think about the jewels, think about the story. When Enrico and I were walking back here tonight, the moon was shining overhead and I knew it was the very same moon that had been shining when the duke lived at the castle. Maybe that moon was watching when he buried his treasure to hide it from the rebellious parliamentarians. And perhaps those Roundheads found the treasure themselves. Maybe some of that wealth helped them overthrow Charles the First. Maybe it was the duke's money that sustained Oliver Cromwell while he ruled. And we're here, where it all happened. We don't need to find the treasure to love the story. Can't you just see that man, riding his stallion?"

Carole shook her head. "There is something wrong there, you know. No horse should be so unmanageable. It's not the horse's fault, either. It's the rider who's to blame when a horse is wild. I bet that man beat his horse. That would explain it. It would make any horse wild and unmanageable. I wish I'd been there. If I'd been there, I would have made him stop hurting the stallion. Then maybe he wouldn't have buried the treasure in the stable and maybe the stallion would have lived and the treasure would have been found—"

"Hold it," Lisa said. "I think we're losing track of what's important here."

"What's that?" asked Carole.

"We can't change the past, so we have to deal with the present. And the present question is what are we going to wear to the ball?"

"Not the duke's jewels, I guess," Stevie conceded.

"I guess you're right about that," said Carole.

"Well, if we don't have jewels and fancy dresses, I think we should go as Roundheads," said Lisa.

"No jewels at all?" Stevie asked. "Not even these?" She jumped off her bed and burrowed through her suitcase. After a few minutes, during which a pile of clothes grew on the floor next to the suitcase, she drew a long string of pearls from the suitcase's side pocket.

"Where did you get those?" Carole asked. She had no idea Stevie had such nice jewelry.

"Oh, the drug store," Stevie said. She draped the pearls over her neck and tugged at them to straighten them out. She tugged too hard, though. The string holding them snapped, and pearls scattered onto the floor and began rolling every which way.

"Wait! I'll help!" said Lisa, diving for an errant pearl headed for a permanent hiding place under the radiator.

"Here are some," said Carole, delivering a handful to Stevie.

"Don't worry, don't worry," Stevie assured them. "I think I paid three dollars and twenty-nine cents for the whole string of them. I'd never wear them. I just thought they were funny."

"Oh," Lisa said, withdrawing her hand from under the radiator. She opened her fist to see if she'd retrieved the pearl, but all she had was a dust bunny.

The girls sat back down on their beds.

"So, Roundheads it is," Stevie said.

"I bet Veronica finds a way to dress as a Cavalier," Carole said.

"I'm sure she will," said Lisa. "The last time I saw her, she was looking for a fax machine!"

Stevie and Carole laughed. It was *so* like Veronica!

"Maybe we should restring these beads and give them to her to wear. We'd have to tell her they are real pearls, though. She'd never wear fakes."

"She wouldn't know a fake if she saw it," Lisa said. "What do you think, Carole?"

Carole didn't answer. She had a faraway look in her eyes.

"Carole? Are you okay?" Stevie asked.

A smile came across Carole's face. "I'm just fine," she assured her friends. "Except that I think I've been spending too much time around a certain Stevie Lake."

"You've got an idea?" Lisa asked.

Carole nodded.

"A *scheme?*" Stevie asked.

"Yes," Carole said. "Now what do you think about this? . . ."

There was a knock at the door.

"Girls! I told you to go to sleep!"

"Yes, Max," they said in a single voice. But they didn't mean it at all.

10

"WATCH OUT!"

"Don't jostle me!"

"Shhh! Here she comes!"

The Saddle Club became silent and stopped moving—which was a good thing, because the three of them were high up in the branches of an old oak tree. Specifically, they were in the branches of the old oak tree that stood near the creekbed that fed the castle's moat.

In just three hours, they would be in the first portion of the mounted games competition, but now they were having fun, serious fun.

The girls had gotten up very early that morning. They'd eaten breakfast quickly and hurried over to the castle, bringing their riding clothes to change into later.

"There are three qualifications," Carole announced when they arrived at the castle. "And Veronica knows them as well as we do. The stable was almost certainly on flat ground. It had to be close to the castle, and it had to be close to a source of water."

"The creek!" said Lisa.

"Yes, the creek," Stevie agreed. "The one that runs by the oak tree."

"Perfect," said Carole.

It was a very logical place for the duke to have put the stable, but perhaps even more important, it was a logical place for Veronica to *think* the duke had his stable. Best of all, there was the oak tree that now held three Saddle Club members, each clutching her mouth to keep from making a sound.

The leaves on Stevie's branch began quivering. Lisa was afraid the branch might be about to break. When she looked, however, she knew it was something else. The branch was quivering because Stevie was laughing hard and silently, and Lisa was afraid she wouldn't be able to contain herself. Lisa frowned at her. Stevie stopped laughing.

IT HAD TO be here, Veronica said to herself. It just had to be. This is a large flat area, big enough for a stable and even some paddocks and a schooling ring—if dukes did that sort of thing back then. I don't know about that, but anyway, the water is here, it's close to the castle. This is it.

91

She stepped back and closed her eyes. In her mind's eye, the stable rose in front of her. She could see it, just exactly as it must have looked three and a half centuries earlier. It was a large stable, large enough to accommodate all the horses the duke owned, and grand enough to accommodate the one he cared the most about. She took a few steps forward, entering her mind's creation. She could almost feel the cool darkness of the imagined stable, then realized it was actually the shade of the big old oak tree above.

The stallion would have had the stall of honor—the one closest to the door and just to the left.

She looked to her left. She could almost see the stall there. It was a commodious box stall. The imagined stall opened out onto a paddock where an uncontrollable horse could have a free run—inside a high fence, of course. Veronica thought she could smell the hay and the pungent scent of horses. Then she realized she *could* smell those things. But it wasn't the duke's horse she smelled. It was the smell from the tent stables just a stone's throw away. But those were now. She was more concerned with *then*.

The stall had to be here. Maybe here, she thought, pointing to areas of the ground. *And the oak has stood guard over the remains of the stable for centuries, protecting the treasure as the stallion once did.*

She was convinced she had the place. It was time to look. Not that she expected to find jewels on her first trip, but she did expect to get some idea of where she should come to dig in the future. Veronica knelt and ran her hands over the ground. She was feeling for unevenness. The earth would have settled around the treasure, and the settling could be apparent even more than three hundred years later. She was pretty sure of that. At least, she was hopeful of it.

Above her, the leaves of the oak rustled. Veronica didn't hear the noise. All her senses were focused on the earth beneath her hands.

"It must be here," she whispered to herself. The leaves above rustled again, as if in answer. "I can just feel it. I know it."

There was a long silence while she studied the ground with her hands and her eyes.

She picked up small clods of earth and turned them in her hand. Stones, pebbles, an acorn or two fell with the dirt. She picked up another handful. She didn't really expect to find anything. It was just that she had this *feeling* about precious jewelry, like a sixth sense. It was here. She shook with excitement.

She sifted another handful of dirt.

Plunk.

She looked to see what had dropped from her hand. It wasn't a stone or an acorn. It was a dark sphere. She picked it up. She brushed the dirt away. It was round, but it wasn't dark. It was white. It was—

"A *pearl!*" she said out loud.

She felt the earth around where she'd found her prize.

Nothing. Some of the horse show's spectators were walking toward her. They mustn't know. If one person knew, then everyone would know. Quickly Veronica stood up. She slipped her find into her pocket. Her eyes darted around. Nobody had seen. Nobody knew. It was her secret —her treasure! She hurried back to her hotel room.

High above, the tree's branches began shaking, its leaves shivering almost hysterically.

"Hook!" whispered Stevie.

"Line!" said Lisa.

"And sinker!" declared Carole.

Three hands met in a triumphant "high fifteen."

"You're a genius!" Lisa told Carole.

"I'm merely a student of the master," Carole said, nodding to Stevie.

"Let's go groom the horses and then watch some of the dressage," Stevie said. "And plan our next step," she added with glee.

The three girls climbed down out of the oak and headed for the stables—a safe distance behind Veronica diAngelo.

11

"I THINK I like the first day of a three-day event the best," said Stevie as the three of them walked along the aisles to where the Dickens horses were stabled.

"Of course you do," said Lisa. "That's because it's the dressage and you're the best at it of the three of us."

"It always amazes me that someone wild and crazy like Stevie can be good at dressage, which takes so much concentration," Carole remarked.

"You think being wild and crazy doesn't take concentration?" Stevie asked. "Just remember how hard you had to think to come up with the treasure scheme."

Carole thought about it and realized that Stevie might just be right. "I guess you've got a point," she said. "It was hard work."

Lisa could see that Pip was peering out over the half door of his stable. She waved a greeting to him. She was pretty sure he nodded back. She thought he was glad to see her. She knew she was glad to see him. She gave his nose a good rub.

The other horses looked curiously at the girls as they arrived. There was a stir of excitement among them as if they knew why they'd come to Cummington and were ready to compete.

The girls each took up a set of grooming tools and got to work. They wanted their horses to look perfect for the mounted games demonstration. When they were done, they went to check their tack. For Lisa this was particularly important. She couldn't afford another mistake with Pip's bit. Everything was fine.

"I think we should tack them up about an hour before we're due to begin," Carole said. "That should leave us enough time to do it absolutely perfectly and still have time to give them a good warm-up before the actual competition."

That decided, they followed the long path through the stable to the competition ring. The stable was a flurry of activity as each competitor tried to groom his or her horse perfectly. The stable lads scurried around, bringing hoof polish to one rider, boot polish to another, brushing, combing, and shining the horses in every stall.

Horses who were finished with their dressage tests were being patted—or scolded. Those that had yet to compete were being encouraged and hugged, as well as shined. Still others, almost ready to enter the ring, were getting their warm-up runs in a small ring attached to the far side of the stabling area. Everywhere something was happening, and it all had to do with horses.

Stevie took Lisa and Carole's hands and gave them a little squeeze. "Isn't it just *wonderful?*" she asked.

They agreed.

The Saddle Club just *loved* it.

They entered the spectator section of the arena and found seats on a bench in a small area designated for competitors.

Carole picked up a copy of the day's program and scanned the list of competitors.

"Who's on now?" she asked.

Stevie squinted to read the number on the back of the rider. "Four eighty-seven," she said.

"Four eighty-seven . . . four eigh— Nigel's coming up after two more competitors!" she said. She showed the program to Lisa and Stevie.

"That's great!" said Lisa. "I bet Sterling will be fabulous!"

Horse number 487 finished his test, and there was a scattering of applause in the arena. Carole and Lisa clapped and then looked at Stevie for an explanation of the lackluster applause for a test that seemed to them to have been very good.

"The horse did everything she asked, but her signals

were very obvious. The use of aids is supposed to be almost invisible to the audience."

"I'm glad we've got you along to explain these things," said Lisa. "Even though I've studied dressage, there's a lot more of it I don't understand than I do. I want to learn a lot watching these riders."

"And that means knowing what to look for. Thanks, Stevie," Carole added. "Oh, here comes two thirty-one."

The next horse entered the arena. Lisa tried to concentrate on what was happening. On one level, it was obvious that the horse was going to go through the exact same set of movements as the previous horse. The program, or test, was identical for all competitors. The horses followed a course of circles, figure eights, reverses, and turns at different gaits. At all times, the judges were looking for manners in the horse and instant response to nearly invisible commands from the riders. It was intricate and intense, but it had to look effortless.

By the time 231 made a final bow to the judges, Lisa realized she was holding her breath. The audience applauded, and so did Lisa.

"That one was better than the last, wasn't he?" she asked when she breathed.

"Yup," Stevie concurred.

The next horse did well, too. Then came Nigel on Sterling.

"This is going to be the best of all," said Lisa.

"We'll see," said Stevie.

Nigel and Sterling entered the ring with a dignified elegance. Sterling was beautiful, there was no doubt about it. Nigel's eyes quickly scanned the competitors' section of the seats, and when he saw The Saddle Club, he winked at them. They waved back discreetly. He drew to a halt in front of the judges and tipped his hat. It was time to begin.

It was immediately clear that dressage wasn't Sterling's event. Nigel's control was smooth and effortless, but Sterling's responses weren't. He made it through the test, but not without protest. The applause was scattered and unenthusiastic, except from The Saddle Club. Their loyalty made them cheer their favorite rider almost raucously.

"What went wrong?" Lisa asked Stevie the moment Nigel and Sterling turned to leave the ring.

"It's not his event," said Stevie.

"Then what's he doing here?" Lisa asked.

"A three-day event is a chance for horses to show off their strengths in different areas," Carole reminded her. "It's a very rare horse that excels in all three. Sterling's a stallion. That means he's going to be feisty and strong-headed. Those skills should stand him in good stead in the next two events—the cross-country and the stadium jumping. But it's exactly that quality that makes the demanding precision of dressage so hard for him."

"Poor Nigel," said Lisa, looking at him as he paused just outside the ring to talk with a man who was standing there. "He must feel awful."

99

"Not at all," said Stevie. "He did a very good job, under the circumstances, and he'll make up for lost scoring on the next two events. Nigel knows it and so do other people who know these events."

"I don't think that man knows it," Lisa said. She pointed to the man talking to Nigel. The man had a very angry look on his face. He was even shaking his fist at Sterling.

"Well, then, that man's a fool," said Stevie.

Nigel, Sterling, and the angry man moved inside the stables, out of the view of The Saddle Club. The next rider entered the ring. The show continued.

An hour and a half later, The Saddle Club plus Veronica (who had arrived late but perfectly groomed) found themselves at the entrance to the show ring. Veronica hadn't offered any excuse for her lateness, and The Saddle Club didn't ask. They already knew. There was a glow of excitement on Veronica's face that only jewels could cause! The girls didn't even look at one another for fear they'd laugh and give themselves away. Besides, there was something more important to think about right then. It was time for the first portion of their mounted games demonstration.

Carole was thrilled to be there, entering the same ring where championship horses had just performed. The crowd seemed as eager to watch them as it had been to see the dressage. They cheered loudly as the teams were introduced.

"Horse Wise, Willow Creek, Virginia, United States of America!" the public address system announced. That was their cue. In they went!

The rules of the demonstration provided that there would be four races on each of the three days of the event. The team that won each race got four points; second place earned three points; third place received two points; and last place just one point. The award would be given on the third day.

The riders didn't know what the races would be. They were explained before each race began. The Saddle Club had talked about the possibilities. Stevie was famous for coming up with wild and crazy horseback relay races. When Stevie was in charge, races were likely to include eggs, squirt guns, buckets of feathers, and Jell-O mold salads. In other words, they were very Stevian. Instead, today's races included flags, batons, and ropes. In other words, they were very normal races. They tested riding skills like speed, accuracy, and the ability to stop and turn. Those were exactly the skills the girls had admired in the horses that Tessa loaned them.

Tessa was there, of course. She and Mrs. Reg were sitting in the competitors' section. They cheered loudly as the girls entered the ring. Max was waiting in the stabling area with the other coaches.

The first race was explained. The first rider had to pick up a flag from the far end of the ring, bring it back, and give it to the second rider, who rode the course, returned, and handed the flag off to the third, who did the same. The fourth rider had to return the flag to the far end and ride back across the finish line.

Stevie led off. Copperfield's speed put their team in front before she'd even picked up the flag, and they were never out of first place. Veronica had no difficulty on Nickleby, even though she'd never ridden him before. Pip behaved like the perfect gentleman he was—when he had the right bit in his mouth—and Carole practically flew through her leg of the race on Miss Havisham. Not only did the team come in first, but they even had time to watch the Dutch and English riders finish up.

"Nice job, Lisa," Enrico said.

"Thanks," she answered.

"But perhaps you will not always come in first," he said, teasing.

"Perhaps," she said, accepting the jest.

The next race was very similar, only this time it was a baton instead of a flag and it didn't go quite as well for the Horse Wise team as the first race had. Stevie knew they were in trouble as soon as the handkerchief dropped and the race started. Copperfield absolutely flew across the starting line. He was so sleek and speedy that riding him was an utter joy. Stopping him was something else. Both Stevie and Copperfield got carried away and overran the course. That put the team behind. They ended up in second place behind the English team. The Italians were third, the Dutch fourth.

The next race was a rope race. This required pairs of riders to circle the course next to one another, holding a short length of rope between them. It meant they had to ride close to one another at exactly the same speed. If one let go of the rope, they both had to stop, return to the place where it happened, and pick up the race again. If they dropped the rope altogether, both riders had to dismount, pick it up, remount, and begin the course again.

Everything started out fine. Stevie's and Veronica's horses matched one another stride for stride, and the first pair returned way ahead of any of the other teams.

Lisa grasped her end of the rope.

"Let's go!" Carole said. They were off.

Lisa and Pip were on the inside. Lisa found that it took an enormous amount of concentration and control to maintain an even pace and stay next to Carole. Pip seemed to think it was a race against Miss Havisham, and he wanted badly to win. Lisa held the reins firmly with one hand and kept him under control while she clutched the rope tightly with the other. It worked for a while, but when they got to the turn, it stopped working. Pip's ability to make tight turns put him way ahead of Miss Havisham at the turn, and try as she did to hold on to the rope and the reins, one had to go. It was the rope. She couldn't stop Pip for another five strides, and then she had to turn him around. Fortunately, Miss Havisham had stopped as soon as the rope had dropped and Carole was waiting for Lisa's return. Lisa came back and took her end of the rope, and there was no more trouble for the rest of the race.

They came in second.

"I'm sorry," Lisa said to Carole.

"Don't worry about it," Carole assured her. "No race is perfect."

But their next one was. It was a simple race of gaits. They were to trot their horses down to the far end and canter them back, no gallop, no walk, just trot and canter. It was a breeze of a race for this foursome. Their horses were well trained and obedient and had fluid, swift gaits. Horse Wise finished the afternoon with the same feeling of satisfaction that they'd had with the first race.

In fact, it seemed as if the hardest thing they had to do was to keep from yelling with joy until they left the ring. They were—all four of them—immensely pleased with themselves and proud of the job they'd done.

"BRILLIANT! YOU WERE all brilliant!" Tessa greeted the Horse Wise riders while they cooled their horses in the paddock by the stable.

"Oh, you're just saying that because they're your horses!" Lisa teased.

"Even the most brilliant horse needs a brilliant rider!" Tessa declared.

Max agreed. He stood next to Tessa, glad of the opportunity to thank her for the loan of the horses.

"You did a good job, girls. I'm proud of the team for winning two races and coming in second two times, but I'm even prouder of the horsemanship and teamwork I saw out there."

"See? Just as I said: Brilliant!" agreed Tessa.

As soon as the horses were cooled, the girls dismounted and walked them back to their stables for a good grooming and a well-deserved snack of hay and water and a few carrots.

The girls slipped out of their riding habits and into jeans for grooming. When they came out of the dressing room, they found some of the lads there, offering to help groom. The Saddle Club demurred. Veronica accepted. She explained that she had an important errand in town and wanted to be sure to get there before the shops closed.

"Do you think she's in such a rush to get to a clothing store?" Tessa asked Lisa as she watched Veronica rush out of the stable.

"More likely hardware or garden supplies," Lisa said.

"To buy some flowers?" asked Tessa.

"No, a shovel," said Lisa with a sly grin. The girls explained that Veronica was in search of a treasure trove.

"The duke's jewels!" Tessa said. "What on earth makes her think she's going to find that after all these centuries?"

"She's already found a piece of it," Lisa explained.

"A pearl," Carole supplied.

"From the Duke of Cummington's cache?" Tessa asked, clearly astonished.

"No, more like the Duke of Woolworth's," said Stevie.

"Oh, dear me, you three have been up to something

and I'm afraid I've missed the best of it," Tessa said, clearly understanding their prank.

"Oh, not necessarily the *best*," said Lisa. "Just the *first*." With that, she put down her currycomb and reached into the pocket of her jeans. She pulled out the rhinestone button she'd picked up from the street when she'd been walking with Enrico.

"What's that?" Stevie asked.

"Well," Lisa said, looking at it carefully. "Right now, it's a rhinestone button, but in a minute—" She leaned over and searched through the grooming bucket until she found what she wanted. She brought out her hoof pick and probed under the rhinestone with the pointed end. There was a small crackling sound and the rhinestone popped out of its plastic bed. "In a minute," she repeated. She reached into her purse, brought out an emery board, and carefully filed the bottom of the rhinestone, removing traces of plastic and glue. "In a minute, we have . . ."

"A diamond!" Stevie declared.

"Perfect," said Carole.

"Brilliant," said Tessa.

"The plot thickens," Lisa said.

They hurried to finish the grooming. They had to be sure to plant the "diamond" before Veronica returned with a shovel.

When the last flake of hay was secured in the horses' stalls, the girls exited the stables and returned to the scene of their crime. The dressage tests had resumed, so all the spectators were in the stands and the grounds of the castle were deserted. The girls slipped the rhinestone under an inch of earth near where they'd put the pearl and looked for a hiding place. The tree was fun, but risky. They were going to have to be farther away. Their only choice was behind the canvas of the stabling tent. They scurried back to the tent, hid themselves, and waited.

"Here comes someone," Stevie whispered.

"Veronica?" Tessa asked.

"I don't think so," said Stevie. "Walking too slowly."

Lisa peered around the tent flap. "Definitely not Veronica," she said. "It's a man and he's got a limp."

"What's he doing?" Carole asked.

"He's looking at the stable," Tessa said.

"Why isn't he looking at the horses in the ring?" Carole asked.

"Not everybody loves dressage," Stevie said.

"Shhh," said Lisa.

"He can't hear us," Stevie said. "And besides, he's walking away."

"Maybe he just took a wrong turn," said Carole.

"Well, he's going now," said Lisa. She watched the man's awkward pace as he followed the road back to town.

For a while nothing happened. Lisa thought maybe Veronica couldn't get a shovel and wouldn't return.

"No way," said Stevie. "I saw that look in her eyes. She'd dig with a spoon if she had to. A silver spoon!"

The girls giggled, but their giggling stopped when Veronica appeared. She had a small garden spade in her hand. She looked around furtively and, seeing no one, began examining the earth under the oak tree carefully.

It didn't take long. She scratched around in the earth for a few minutes with the spade. Then she stopped suddenly.

"We've got her!" Stevie whispered.

"Shhh," the three other girls answered.

Veronica reached down to the ground. She picked up something. She looked at it. She caressed it. She looked around and, seeing she was alone, stuck the object in her pocket. She grabbed her shovel and ran back toward the town.

"Perfect!" Stevie declared, and nobody could disagree. The girls collapsed into giggles in the stable tent.

"But what comes next?" Stevie asked.

"Probably earth-moving equipment!" Carole said.

"Oh, not yet. This is too much fun. Do you think we could find an opal or an emerald or a ruby?" Stevie said.

"Not likely," said Lisa.

"I say, have you girls ever heard of something called pyrite?" Tessa asked.

"*Fool's gold!*" Stevie said. "Can you get some?"

"Well, my brother has a mineral collection. I don't suppose he'd miss a very small chunk off of his pyrite," said Tessa.

"You mean you'd steal from your brother just for this?" Lisa asked.

"Of course!" Tessa responded.

"Aren't brothers wonderful?" Stevie said, giving Tessa a glance of renewed admiration.

That was the only time Lisa and Carole had ever heard her express such an idea, and they told her so.

"Well, now I know for sure that being willing to steal something from a brother doesn't keep one from being a lady!" Stevie exclaimed with glee.

"Not at all," Tessa agreed conspiratorially. "I'll do the deed tonight at home and then bring it back tomorrow."

Lisa looked at Carole and Stevie. "Didn't I tell you she was wonderful?"

Nigel Hawthorne sat proudly at the head of the table. He was having dinner with the Horse Wise team and seemed very pleased to have the four girls as his guests. He had wanted to include Tessa in the invitation, but she'd had to get back to Dickens. She had a very important errand there.

"Oh, do have another slice," he said to Stevie.

"Thank you, Nigel, but I couldn't," Stevie said, more truthfully than she and her friends wanted to admit.

"Well, I know Americans think theirs is the best pizza in the world, but I thought you'd like to have a taste of English-style pizza while you're here."

Veronica started to say something. Carole didn't like the look on her face, so she started talking instead.

"It's delicious," she assured him. "It's just that all the excitement of the show and all—you know."

"Oh, I do," Nigel said, taking another slice of pepperoni pizza for himself. "I must say, aside from watching your team perform brilliantly, my favorite part of the day was hearing my personal fan club cheer me from the competitors' section."

"Were we clapping too loudly?" Stevie asked.

"Not at all," said Nigel. "I truly appreciated it. In fact, it seemed as if it was the only appreciation I got all day."

Carole remembered the man who had greeted Nigel so unpleasantly at the exit gate of the arena. "Was that Lord Yaw—what's his name?"

"Just call him Yaxley," Nigel said. "And yes, it was. He's none too happy with me and Sterling."

"But you were wonderful and Sterling was doing his best," Stevie said.

"Apparently my wonderful and Sterling's best are not good enough for Yaxley. He explained to me in clear tones that he'd been hoping for better."

"He's tougher than *Max*," Carole said.

Nigel laughed. "Much. And more unreasonable, too. Still, I reminded him that dressage isn't Sterling's event. He'll do better tomorrow, and better still in the jumping. A stallion like Sterling is too high-strung for the discipline of dressage."

"And we'll cheer for him even more loudly, then," Lisa promised.

"I'll be listening for it," Nigel said. "And I'll be cheering for Horse Wise at the mounted games, as well." Nigel lifted his glass to the team, and they lifted theirs to him. Veronica didn't say a word about English pizza—or any other pizza. Any time Veronica didn't say something was a good time as far as The Saddle Club was concerned.

When dinner was finished, Carole asked Nigel if he could drop them off at the stables so that they could be sure their horses were properly bedded down for the night.

"I'd be pleased to do that. I wish I could come with you, but my own team is having a meeting. I have an early start time tomorrow. Will you look in on Sterling while you're there?"

"Definitely," Carole said. "In fact, I brought an extra carrot just for him."

Nigel led the girls to his car. "Next stop, the stable."

"Could you just drop me at the hotel?" Veronica asked. "I have a little more confidence in the lads at the stable than my teammates do, and I'm so tired . . ." She stretched her arms out as if to prove a point that nobody believed anyway.

A few minutes later, Stevie, Lisa, and Carole hopped out of Nigel's car at the stable, thanking him sincerely for a wonderful dinner and the ride.

"See you tomorrow!" Nigel said.

"Good luck!" called Stevie. Nigel waved and off he went.

The long summer twilight was finally turning to darkness as the girls entered the stable tent. 'Ank sat with his feet propped up on his desk, sound asleep. Behind him, a horse snorted. 'Ank woke up with a start.

"Well, what are you doing 'ere?" he demanded when he saw the three girls in front of him.

"Just checking on our horses," Lisa said.

"Ay, the Dickens 'orses, Oi remember," he said. "You know the way. Get on with it."

The girls took that as permission and made their way down the aisle. Their first stop was Sterling. He seemed relaxed, as if he knew that the hardest part of the event was over for him.

Carole slipped him his carrot and patted him. He remained aloof, as if seeming grateful were undignified.

"Oh, come on, boy. Everybody loves a carrot!" Carole teased. She held out her hand to pat him. Finally he gave in. He stepped over to the door of the stall and allowed Carole to give him a pat and then a hug. Then, as if he were embarrassed by his show of affection, he stepped back into the corner of the stall.

"Good night," Carole said. She turned to her friends. "He's just bashful," she explained. Lisa and Stevie agreed.

Their next stop was to check on their own horses. They were fine and in good spirits and all welcomed the late-night snack. Nickleby enjoyed his as much as the others did.

"We're sorry you got Veronica," Stevie said. "She's too selfish to come here herself, but we promise to take as good care of you as we do the other horses. We've gotten good at making up for her shortcomings!" Nickleby seemed unconcerned. He was just happy to have a sweet carrot to munch.

"I think it's time to get back," Lisa said. "We've got to work out our costumes for tomorrow night."

"Oh, right. It's only Veronica who is having something expressed across the Atlantic, isn't it? We have to *do* something." Stevie sighed.

"Okay, let's go," Carole said, giving Miss Havisham a final pat.

They said good night to 'Ank and began the pleasant walk back to their hotel. The girls chatted about their costumes as they walked, trying to decide exactly what to do with their hair so that they'd look like Roundheads.

"Mousse," said Stevie. "That can hold it flat."

"Gel," Carole suggested.

"Why don't we just wear ponytails?" Lisa asked. "I don't think they had mousse in the sixteen-forties."

"But they had greasy stuff. I'm sure," Carole said.

"Did you bring some gel?" Stevie asked.

"Uck, no. I hate the stuff," said Carole.

"I do, too, but I brought it anyway," said Stevie.

"I brought mousse," Lisa said. "But I still think ponytails will do it—as long as we can make our hair lie flat."

"Look, here's what we can do," Stevie said. She wanted to demonstrate how to brush and comb their hair so that it would come out perfectly. She stepped in front of her friends and began walking backward rapidly so that they could see what she was doing.

"If we brush it upwards and then—"

She didn't mean to walk right into the man in the trench coat, but she never saw him, and because he had a limp he couldn't get out of the way fast enough.

Both of them fell to the ground. Stevie popped right up.

"Oh, I'm sorry!" she said.

The man just grumbled as he struggled to right himself.

"Here, I'll help you," Stevie said, offering him a hand. He took it grudgingly.

"I really didn't mean to do that," Stevie said.

The man just glared. Then he limped on slowly. He never said a thing to Stevie.

"How rude," Stevie muttered as the girls continued their walk.

Carole and Lisa agreed. Even though Stevie shouldn't have bumped into him, she had helped him up and had apologized.

"Some people," Stevie said finally.

"Some people shouldn't walk backwards in the dark," Carole said.

"I know," Stevie conceded. "But I do have this great idea for our hair. Still, I guess I'm going to have to wait until we're back in the room."

A few minutes later in their hotel room, Stevie had the

116

chance to demonstrate. It involved ponytails, gel, and mousse.

"It looks pretty awful, but very roundheaded," Lisa admitted.

By the time Stevie was finished with her hairdressing demonstration, Lisa had assembled an outfit that would work for all of them. "If we go as boys—you know, the apprentices who were the first ones to sign up with the Roundheads—then we can really just wear our riding clothes, breeches, high boots, loose blouses, and no jackets."

"And then if we get a chance to buy some orange ribbon, we can add orange sashes. That was what the Roundhead soldiers wore," said Carole.

"Perfect," Lisa agreed. "And that's that."

"Except for masks," Stevie said. "What are we going to do for masks?"

"Do you think we could get hold of some Groucho glasses—you know, nose and mustache?" Carole asked.

"Not what I had in mind," said Stevie. "For this kind of costume ball, you're supposed to have the kind of mask that you sort of hold up to your face." She scrunched her face in thought. "If only we had some cardboard—any cardboard." Then her eyes came to rest on the desk, where a booklet about the hotel's amenities lay. "Ah!" she said. "The room service menu!"

Ten minutes later, each girl had a small mask cut from

the room service menu. Lisa and Carole agreed that nobody but Stevie would have thought of that.

"A good night's work," Stevie declared.

Her friends agreed. It was time to sleep. Tomorrow would be another very busy day.

* * *

Cummington Castle
July 20

Dear Diary,

Today I found the first of the duke's treasure. I truly did! I can hardly believe it myself, but here, sitting in front of me, are two jewels, a pearl and a diamond. There's only one explanation for their presence under the oak tree by the castle. And this is just the tip of the iceberg! I'm bursting to tell somebody, but I can't. It has to be my secret until I've found it all, every last gem. I can't wait!

Speaking of things I can't wait for, tomorrow's ball is one of them. My dress will arrive tomorrow. The poor other Pony Clubbers who won't have proper ballgowns will have to go as boring old Roundheads. I shall be a glamorous Cavalier and I intend to look the part. My appearance will surely appeal most to one who is used to fine and beautiful things. And won't he just love the tiara?!!!!

Love, soon-to-be-rich-even-beyond-my-wildest-dreams,
Veronica

118

14

"COME ON, LET'S get going. No dawdling," Carole said the next morning, sounding more like a parent than she'd meant to. She herded her two friends through the village and over to the stables. "We don't have any time to waste."

"For someone who can be flaky about a lot of things, you certainly are being organized this morning," Stevie said, trailing after her friend.

"We have to be there for Nigel," Carole reminded Stevie and Lisa. "He said he's got an early start time for the cross-country jumping and he needs us to cheer him on. We can't let him down!"

Lisa and Stevie both began walking faster.

They found Nigel at Sterling's stall, doing a final check on the stallion's grooming. Standing next to him was the man they knew was Yaxley. He didn't seem any happier this morning than he had been yesterday afternoon. The girls didn't want to get in the way. They stood nearby, trying to appear as if they weren't listening. Yaxley paid no attention to them. He just scowled while Nigel talked, and nothing Nigel said seemed to please him.

"We'll do our best, sir," Nigel said.

"Your best wasn't good enough yesterday," Yaxley grumbled.

"Dressage isn't Sterling's event," Nigel said. "He's too spirited for it."

"And what about today's cross-country? What are you going to be saying to me after that?"

"I'm going to be saying that we've done our best, sir," Nigel said.

"Hmph," Yaxley remarked. Then he stomped off.

"How can you stand that?" Stevie asked Nigel when she was pretty sure Yaxley was out of earshot.

"It's the price I pay for being able to ride a fabulous horse like Sterling. It's not the stallion's fault that his owner is a wretch."

Carole rubbed her hand along the horse's face. He responded by nodding, as if he remembered the carrot she'd brought him the night before.

"How strange to have such a dreadful man own such a

wonderful horse," she said, smoothing the stallion's silvery coat.

"In a way, I understand," Nigel said. "Horses are a business for him and he sees this fellow as an investment—an expensive one. He had his hopes set on Sterling."

"As a show horse?" Stevie asked.

"No, as a breeder. But to be a valuable breeder, the horse first has to show that he's got the stuff of champions. Unless he does, he'll never be a valuable stallion because the public will not be clamoring for his offspring. I want the horse to succeed, but I also want to succeed for Yaxley. Years ago, he was one of the first owners to let me ride his mounts in the competition ring. I owe him a lot."

"Well, you're giving him a lot, too," Carole said. "And I don't think he understands how much."

"He doesn't have to understand, really. It's my job to win for him."

"And we'll be cheering you on, too!" Lisa said brightly.

"Where are you going to be on the course?" Nigel asked.

"Everywhere," Stevie assured him. She pulled a course map out of her pocket and showed him how they'd all figured they could dash around the course and watch Nigel several times during his trial. "We call these checkpoints," Stevie explained. "If we've got the timing right, we should be able to see you in the woods, in the swamp, and at three jumps that are near each other."

"Plus at the finish, of course," Carole said.

"Every time you hear cheers, it's us," Lisa promised.

"So good luck!" Carole said. The girls gave Nigel and Sterling final pats and hugs.

"Thanks, girls," Nigel said. "Your support means a great deal to me—"

"And to Sterling?" Carole asked.

"And to Sterling," Nigel assured them.

The Saddle Club had seen cross-country courses before, but they'd never seen one this rigorous. Pine Hollow sponsored a three-day event every year, but three-day events varied tremendously in their difficulty, particularly in the cross-country section. In this case, the course was expected to take each rider about fifteen minutes to complete, including a section through a hilly wooded area, one through a swampy section, and another, the easiest to watch, over a serpentine of hazardous jumps. It was expected to be exhausting to the rider and the horse. One look at the first few riders covering the course and the girls knew that these expectations were completely accurate.

"First stop: the hillside!" Stevie declared and then led the way.

"This can't be right," said Lisa a while later when Stevie stopped to check her map. They were standing at the base of what seemed almost like a cliff—a rocky obstacle perhaps five feet high—leading up to a path that snaked through the woods.

"No way," Carole agreed.

Twenty minutes later, the first horse arrived. The rider, seeing what lay ahead, took a good running start, and up the horse went, scrambling up the cliff onto the trail.

"Whew!" said Carole. "I'm not sure I would have thought it was possible."

"What number was that?" Lisa asked.

"Seven-oh-six," Carole said.

"Two more and then Nigel."

The next competitor appeared a little while later. As with the previous one, the rider decided that the way to get up the hill was at a gallop. The horse agreed. They reached the base of the cliff and the horse crested it in two long strides. Unfortunately, the rider didn't make it at all. She remained on the ground below, stunned by her fall.

She shook her head to clear it. Then she tried to stand up. Her ankle collapsed under her and she fell again.

She was out of the race and the competition. An official retrieved her horse while a medic helped her off the course and into an ambulance.

It was a sobering scene that prepared them for what was to come. The next horse refused the obstacle repeatedly, and he and his rider were eliminated.

Then came Nigel. Lisa and Stevie held their breath as they watched Nigel. Carole didn't take her eyes off Sterling. The horse's muscles shivered with anticipation. His nostrils flared. His gait changed from an easy canter to a tearing gallop. His head came forward, chin jutting almost

123

determinedly. His ears lay back. His tail flicked. He was ready. He never hesitated as he approached the cliff and he simply flew upward, landing smoothly on the ground above. Nigel beamed with pride.

"Yoweeeee!" Stevie cried out. Carole and Lisa joined her in cheering on their favorite rider. Nigel and Sterling were magnificent. And then they were gone, dashing along the course to their next obstacle.

Stevie checked her map. Their next checkpoint was on the other side of the hill. The girls ran around the hill as quickly as they could, arriving at the swampy area just in time to see the white stallion sloshing through the water at a raging clip.

The girls had to hurry to get to their next checkpoint so that they could watch Sterling jump.

It took them several minutes to make it back to the jump serpentine. By then they were tired from jogging, taking shortcuts across the course. The horses and riders had gone the long way at a gallop most of the time and had to be near exhaustion. And then they had to jump. The girls couldn't wait to see how Nigel and Sterling did.

Just as they found a perch where they could view three of the jumps on the course, horses started thundering through one at a time. The horse before 706 arrived, splattering mud everywhere.

"This isn't a neat and tidy event, is it?" Lisa asked, removing a gob of mud from her forehead.

"No, it's pure rough-and-tumble," Carole said, grinning with excitement.

The first jump they could see appeared to be a regular white fence. However, on the far side of it was a small pool of water. The horses would land in the water and then scramble up out of the pool.

"That's one way of getting the mud off," said Stevie, wiping splashed water off her course map.

By the time they'd dried themselves off, horse number 706 was ready to soak them again. They'd gotten smarter, however, and were now standing back a few feet. It was a good thing, because 706 was a magnificent jumper and soared right over the fence. His splash was tremendous. Apparently the rider was unaware of the water; she shrieked in surprise. The horse, however, was unflappable. He just kept on going.

"That's a great horse," said Carole.

"Not a bad rider," Stevie said.

"What a pair!" Lisa said, smiling to herself. She was feeling wonderful. There she was with her two best friends, watching beautiful horses do seemingly impossible things. It was a nearly perfect combination. Only one thing could make it better.

"Here comes Nigel!" Stevie announced.

A look at Sterling made the girls realize that number 706 had been merely a horse. Sterling was a magnificent steed.

Nigel approached the jump at a smooth speed and at

just the right instant signaled Sterling to jump. The stallion flicked his tail, rose in the air, and soared over the jump. He flew so well and so far that he landed on the other side of the water. He never splashed a drop.

"That ought to keep Yaxley happy!" Stevie said.

"Yeah," said Carole.

Minutes later Sterling and Nigel reappeared, ready for the next jump in their view.

"I don't think I've ever seen jumping like that," Carole said, watching him take the next jump. Sterling made it over, but he stumbled as he landed. Clearly he was getting tired. He refused the third jump once, but flew right over it on the next try. And then it was time for the girls to race to the finish line.

The last part of the course was open and flat except for a final triple combination of jumps right before the finish line. The Saddle Club found Max, Mrs. Reg, Veronica, and Tessa waiting for them. Tessa winked as The Saddle Club arrived in the stands. Stevie knew the signal. It meant she had the pyrite. The three girls joined their group and waited for Nigel and Sterling's finish.

"Where have you been?" Veronica asked.

"Out on the course watching Nigel," Carole said.

"How's he doing?" Max asked.

"Brilliantly," Lisa told him.

"Well, we did see Sterling refuse a jump, but he made it the next try," said Carole.

126

"That can happen on a cross-country course like this," Max said.

"Here he comes!" Stevie announced, spotting the speeding silvery horse.

The actions of the horse and rider were so smooth as they cantered that Nigel and Sterling seemed to flow across the final mile of the course rather than ride it. No matter how tired the horse was, his motion appeared effortless. Carole hoped that would be true of the final jumps as well.

Then the pair entered the ring where the course ended. Sterling didn't hesitate at the final triple jump. His pace never slowed. He attacked the obstacle with courage. His feet ticked the first of the jumps, but it stayed up. He knocked the second one down but managed the third one without trouble. Then, clearly near exhaustion, they crossed the finish line.

Nigel's personal cheering section rose to its feet and clapped as loudly as they could while the rider drew to a halt and bowed to the judges' box. He then tipped his hat to the Pine Hollow group.

Lisa looked up at the scoreboard where Nigel's score was posted. A cross-country event such as this was scored for time and faults. As long as a rider came in within the prescribed time, there were no time faults. In general, the time allowance was intended to be sufficient. Most riders who weren't making egregious mistakes would make it within the time limit. So the more important factor became faults earned along the course. Faults would be given if a horse refused a jump, if the rider took him off the course, if the horse or the rider or both fell, and for many other things. Because of the length and difficulty of the course, it was virtually impossible for a rider to have a clear round with no faults.

Nigel hadn't had a clear round because of Sterling's refusal and knocking one jump down, but he'd had a pretty good round and his fans were proud of him.

"He's in second place!" Lisa said, looking up at the board.

"But it's early in the day," Carole reminded her. There are a lot of other riders yet to come."

"Still, I bet Yaxley will be happy with these results," Lisa said.

"He should be," Max said.

"He should have been happy yesterday, too, but he wasn't," Stevie told Max.

"Well, I was happy with the way my group performed yesterday," Max said. "And I'll be happy today, too, *if* everybody is ready on time." Max looked at his watch. It was a clear sign that it was definitely time to get to work grooming and tacking up.

"Race you to the stables!" Stevie said. The Saddle Club ran off. Veronica followed them at a leisurely walk.

15

"ALL RIGHT, EVERYBODY ready?"

They all were. Sixteen Pony Club riders were set for the next round of games.

"Then *smile!*" the woman commanded brightly before she opened the gate to let them into the ring.

Lisa, Stevie, Carole, and Veronica all smiled confidently. They had a lot to smile about—they were in first place. When Lisa thought back on that moment later, she realized it was probably the last time that afternoon that she'd smiled.

Nothing went right for the team from the moment the first handkerchief dropped until the final points were awarded. It wasn't any one person's fault, either. They were all making terrible mistakes.

Stevie got mixed up and carried the batons both ways instead of handing them off to Carole in the first race. That earned the team a fourth place. In the second race, it was Lisa's turn to blow it. She and Pip circled the pole in the wrong direction and had to go back and circle it again. That moved them from first to third in the race. In the third race, Stevie dropped her egg three times. That wouldn't have been so bad, because all the teams dropped their eggs. It was hard to hold an egg in a spoon on horseback. The really bad part was when Carole dropped it and Miss Havisham stepped on it. When Carole dismounted to fetch the egg, it was scrambled. Third place.

The team was drawing attention from the crowd, who wanted to see what kind of awful mistake they would make in the final race. The crowd was not disappointed. In the fourth race, it was Veronica's turn to goof. She spilled an entire bucket of water, mostly on herself. At first there were just titters from the audience. Then, as Veronica tried to refill the bucket from the spigot, Nickleby got into the act. Apparently all that running and racing had made him thirsty, because as quickly as Veronica filled the bucket, he emptied it. When she bent to pick it up, he'd drained it nearly dry. The audience began laughing out loud.

By the time Veronica had actually filled the bucket, returned to the course, and completed it, handing the bucket to Lisa, the whole race was lost. Good sportsmanship required that the team finish the race, and the only way to do that was to pretend nothing was wrong. By the time Lisa took the course, all the other teams had finished. Nevertheless, she and Pip did a good job, and after them Carole and Miss Havisham did a great job. The result of that was that when Carole finally finished, the team got a standing ovation. That felt good. The fourth place they took for the day did not.

"Oh, that was awful!" Stevie groaned while they were untacking their horses and getting ready to groom them.

The Italian team walked past their stalls.

"Better luck tomorrow," said Gian.

"Though not so much luck that you beat us again as you did yesterday," Marco added.

"Don't worry," Stevie said. "Tomorrow we're going to beat you better than we did yesterday!"

"We shall see!" Marco said.

"Can you teach me some of your techniques?" Andre asked the girls, innocently. "I'd like to pass them on to all our opponents!" The boys laughed.

The girls knew the boys were just teasing, but still it hurt a little. Nobody liked being embarrassed by their own performance.

"Oh, come on," Carole said to her teammates. "Everybody has bad days."

"This wasn't just bad," Stevie said, hefting Copperfield's saddle off his back. "This was *worst*."

"Then tomorrow will be better," Carole said confidently. "It has to be."

"Maybe," said Lisa. "If only we remember what it is we're supposed to do!" She picked up a currycomb and began working on Pip's coat.

"Don't worry, Pip. I'm not mad at you," Lisa said. "The mistakes were all my fault, not yours. You deserve a better rider."

"Oh, you all were wonderful!" came a bright greeting. It was Tessa.

"Were you in the audience?" Stevie asked, genuinely wondering if Tessa had seen the debacle.

"Oh, yes. Everything went wrong, didn't it? Well, that happens to everybody. And tomorrow it can just happen to somebody else. Anyway, the audience loved you."

"They root for underdogs," Lisa said. "We weren't supposed to be an underdog. We started out the day as top dog. I like that better. Can you hand me the dandy brush?"

"I don't know what kind of dog you were, but when things went wrong, you all showed real gumption and courage to continue. Veronica, that was especially true of you."

Veronica looked up, surprised. She was used to getting compliments, but they usually had to do with her hair or her clothes, not her behavior and her spirit. Still, she seemed to know exactly how to respond.

"Breeding will tell," she said. Then she handed Nickleby's lead rope to a lad and walked off, leaving four girls behind her with their jaws agape.

When she could talk, Stevie said, "In her case, I'd like to say the breeding took place in a pigsty, but I don't want to insult pigs!"

The girls finished grooming their horses. Tessa pitched in and did the work on Nickleby. Then, when the horses had been fed and watered, the girls secured them in their stalls. They wanted to get back out to the course to watch the rest of the cross-country trials.

"Come on, this way," Stevie said, leading them through the maze of stalls. The route she chose went near enough to the area where the Italian team's horses were housed that the girls saw something surprising. The boys were all there, finishing the necessary grooming and horse care. Someone else was there, too. Veronica diAngelo.

She stood right next to the door of Enrico's horse's stall. She was peering over the doorway, watching Enrico work and chatting easily with him.

"Oh, you were very courageous to finish the race in that manner," Lisa heard Enrico tell Veronica.

"It seemed to me the only choice I had," Veronica said. "After all, one must maintain one's dignity, don't you think?"

"Definitely," Enrico said. "And you did a fine job of that."

Lisa felt a miserable tightening in her stomach. Enrico was saying nice things—*to Veronica*! When the boys had stopped by their stalls, there had been nothing but teasing. Now he was all sweet and pleasant—*to Veronica*!

"Did you just growl?" Stevie asked Lisa.

"Perhaps," she answered somewhat enigmatically.

"Let's go *this* way," Tessa said, leading the three girls in another direction. Lisa followed blindly.

"Which part of the course do you want to go to first?" Stevie said, unfolding her course map.

"First we have another stop," said Tessa. She patted her pocket significantly.

"Aha!" said Stevie. "You got the goods."

"I did, and I'm certain my brother will never know."

Instead of following the crowd toward the cross-country course, the group followed Stevie to the old oak tree. There was no one around when they reached it. Everybody wanted to watch the competition.

"Lisa, why don't you do the honors?" Tessa invited her.

Lisa wasn't feeling very cheerful or conspiratorial.

"That's okay. You do it," she said.

"No," Carole said. "*You* do it, Lisa. Remember, this isn't just another get-Veronica scheme now. It's a how-can-we-get-even-with-the-rotten-miserable-girl-who's-try-ing-to-steal-your-boyfriend scheme."

A small smile crossed Lisa's face. She held out her hand. "I'll take that fool's gold now," she said.

Tessa handed it to her.

Lisa dropped to her hands and knees and scratched at the earth with her fingernails. In a few minutes, the deed was done. Part three of the duke's treasure was properly placed. She had to bury it a little more deeply than the earlier "treasures" because their afternoon and evening schedules were so busy that Veronica probably wouldn't have a chance to look for it until that night. The last thing they wanted was to have some other spectator come up with the little chunk of pyrite.

Lisa stood up. She didn't know what magic Veronica might work with Enrico, but she knew The Saddle Club was working some very special magic with Veronica.

"Yes, indeed," Lisa announced. "Breeding will tell!"

They headed for the cross-country course to watch another afternoon of exciting riding.

16

"Wow! Did you see that?" Lisa asked. She and her friends were standing on the cross-country course by the jump serpentine. By the time all the horses reached this point, they were tired from the long and arduous course that preceded it. But many of them simply flew over the fences. Sterling had been good. That afternoon the girls found themselves watching a lot of horses that were simply better.

"Watch this man's form," Carole said. "See how he leans into the jump but never loses control or balance?"

"Is that the way I'm supposed to do it?" Lisa asked.

"It's the way everybody's supposed to do it," Tessa said. "Only a few of us are anywhere near that good."

"Including Nigel?" Lisa asked.

"Nigel's that good, sure," Stevie said. "But it's a partnership between the horse and the rider. It has to be just right."

"I guess Sterling is a difficult horse," Lisa said.

"He is," Carole agreed. "But he's got heart and he wants to do his best. He was about ready to collapse this morning, but he kept on going because Nigel asked him to."

For a few minutes, there was no horse on the course. The girls sat down so they could chat.

"Do you ever wonder what the Duke of Cummington's stallion looked like?" Lisa asked her friends.

"Easy," said Carole. "He looked just like Sterling. I knew it the minute I laid eyes on him."

"I think so, too," Lisa agreed. She pulled a blade of grass and began to chew on it. "Do you think Sterling's got a secret like the duke's stallion did?"

"You mean like a treasure that can only be found by a rider with fire in his heart?" Tessa asked, echoing the words of the story 'Ank had told to Lisa and Enrico.

"I guess that's what I mean," Lisa said.

"Depends on what you mean by treasure," said Carole.

"Or what you mean by fire," said Tessa.

That made Lisa think. She considered the romantic fable and remembered that there was a lot of fire in it. There was the fire of passion that the duke had for Lady Elizabeth; there was the fire that burned the stable and consumed the stallion; and there was the fire opal he held in his hand—the only part of his treasure anyone had ever found.

Carole was thinking as well. "All horses have secrets," she said. "They try to share them with us, but they can't always succeed. It's the rider's job to find out what's in her horse's heart. That is the key to the union of horse and rider. Think about the contestants we've seen this afternoon. With the best of them, it's almost impossible to tell where the rider ends and the horse begins. It's as if they're one and the same."

"Maybe you're right," Lisa said.

"Oh, here comes another," Tessa said, watching the next contestant emerge from the forest. The girls stood up and watched.

It was nearly impossible to watch the competitors without comparing them to Nigel. This one wasn't as good a rider as Nigel, but the horse was making a smoother run on the course than Sterling.

"I bet they got more penalty points than Nigel," Carole said.

"Maybe," Tessa agreed.

Then another rider came along the course. "Lots more penalty points," Lisa said. She hoped she was right.

By the time the final rider was nearing the end of the course, the girls were almost as tired as the competitors. They headed for the finish line to see the final standings. Nigel and Sterling were no longer in second place. They had fallen to ninth. In the large field of competitors, that was an excellent finish, and the girls were rightly proud of their friend Nigel.

"But that's not good enough for a championship, is it?" Lisa asked.

"No," Carole agreed. "And perhaps more to the point, it's not going to be good enough for that man Yaxley, either."

"But it's good enough for us, isn't it?" Lisa asked. "Nigel's done a wonderful job and I'm proud to be in his cheering section."

"Prouder than he was to be in ours this afternoon," Stevie said, reminding her friends of the humiliation they'd met in the mounted games.

"Oh, let's change the subject," Tessa said wisely. "Why don't we go and get ready for the ball? I had Hamilton drop my suitcase off at your hotel this morning. You've got space enough for me to spend the night in your room, don't you?"

"We'll make space," Carole assured her.

The girls made a final check of their own horses and headed back to the hotel. Carole, Stevie, and Tessa went straight upstairs. Lisa volunteered to shop for orange sashes in downtown Cummington.

It didn't take long to find the right place. Cummington had a Marks & Spencer's right on the High Street. Lisa loved the store. It had everything from handbags to frozen food, plus makeup, books, fabric, and notions. In fifteen minutes, she'd secured enough bright orange ribbon to make Roundhead sashes for herself and her friends. She paid the cashier and headed back to the hotel.

Lisa had only been on the streets of Cummington with Enrico or with her friends. Now she was alone, and this gave her a real chance to look at the town. It was old. The main street still had cobblestones, and many of the buildings that edged High Street had been there for more than two hundred years. Lisa thought the town probably didn't look very different from the way it did when the duke owned all the lands around. She could almost hear the hooves of his stallion clopping down High Street. The thought made her smile.

In Willow Creek, anything over a hundred years old was an antique. Here, a hundred years was still new. Parts of the castle were known to be more than five hundred years old. Parts of this town were probably that old as well.

Lisa took a deep breath of air, thinking that perhaps she was breathing the same air the duke had breathed those hundreds of years earlier.

In an alley just off High Street, there was an old building made of stone with small-paned windows. It looked as if it had been there as long as the castle. As Lisa admired the weathered facade, she saw a man come out of the door, saying something loudly to people still inside. That was when Lisa realized it was a pub, what people back home would have called a bar or a saloon. A big sign swung outside over the door.

"King's Arms," it read. That sounded old, too.

Lisa walked down the alley to get a closer look at the building and the pub. As she stood in front of it, the door swung open again and a well-dressed young man held the door while his companion, a woman, pulled on a sweater. Lisa looked past them. She didn't mean to stare, but she couldn't help herself.

There, standing at the bar, was none other than Lord Yaxley. He looked different from the glowering man Lisa had seen that morning in the stable. For one thing, he had a pint of ale in his hand. For another, there was a smile on his face.

Yaxley had his arm slung across the shoulder of another man at the bar, who stood with his back to Lisa. The other man shifted uneasily, clearly uncomfortable. One leg was held in an awkward position, as if it had been injured. Lisa thought it was just like Yaxley, smiling or not, to let someone with a bad leg stand while Yaxley drank instead of taking the man to a table where he'd be more comfortable.

The woman finished putting on her sweater and stepped out of the pub. The young man let the door swing closed.

It was time to return to the hotel and get dressed.

141

"OH, TESSA!" STEVIE gushed, looking at the dress Tessa took out of a garment bag.

"That's spectacular!" Carole chimed in.

"We're going to look so plain next to you!" Lisa said.

"But that's the idea, isn't it?" Tessa asked. "We've got the excesses of the Cavaliers next to the proper modesty of the Roundheads. Remember, in the end, it was the Roundheads who won the war."

"So then why are you going as a Cavalier?" Stevie asked.

"For one thing, I have the dress. It's my mother's. She had it made for another Civil War ball and I just thought it would be fun to wear it. For another, I have to confess that my family was on the side of the king in this little dispute. I wouldn't want to deceive anyone about that."

"You won't," Lisa assured her. "It will be clear to everyone. Breeding tells, don't you know?"

All four girls burst into laughter. It was always fun to laugh at Veronica's expense.

Lisa picked up her comb, made a small ponytail at the nape of her neck, and started applying mousse to make her hair lie flat on her head.

"I'll take the gel," Stevie said, joining Lisa at the mirror.

"I'll take both," said Carole.

Fifteen minutes later, the girls were ready. The Americans looked properly somber in their riding breeches, boots, and white blouses, but festively adorned with their orange sashes. Tessa looked wonderful. She'd piled her curls up on the top of her head and they tumbled softly down, framing her delicate face.

Lisa looked at her and then crumpled her brow in thought. After a while she spoke. "You look just like the pictures I've seen of Charles the First," she declared.

Tessa glanced in the mirror. "Before he was beheaded, right?" she asked.

Lisa laughed. "Definitely," she assured Tessa.

"Then let's go," Carole said. She looked at her watch. "We're meeting Max, Mrs. Reg, and Veronica in the lobby in three minutes."

Stevie handed each of the girls her mask, cut from the

room service menu and attached at one end to a pencil so
that the girls could hold them up in front of their faces—
as if they'd fool anyone. Tessa had a mask that matched
the green silk fabric of her dress, but she thought the
room service menu masks were much nicer and asked
Stevie to make her one, too. It took Stevie exactly two
minutes.

They each took one last look in the mirror, and then
they were off.

Max and Mrs. Reg were modestly dressed in good party
clothes, neither Roundhead nor Cavalier. Veronica
looked more like an American Civil War belle than a
Cavalier, but she did look fancy.

"Very nice," Tessa said graciously.

"Daddy sent it over to me," Veronica explained. "It
arrived this afternoon by courier. Daddy sent the jewels,
too," she added unnecessarily.

"I think it's time to go," Stevie said pointedly. She was
a bit afraid that Veronica would be inspired to tell Tessa
exactly where her family had bought all the parts of her
outfit—and how much they cost. "Time to hide!" Stevie
declared. All four girls held their room service menu
masks to their faces. Max and Mrs. Reg burst into laughter. Veronica laughed, too, but her laugh was more one of
disdain than pleasure. That was just the reaction Stevie
had expected.

The group walked over to the castle.

This was the first time the girls had actually been inside

the duke's home. They entered the gates of the castle, crossing the moat. That brought them into the castle courtyard. The main castle was straight ahead.

"His servants and soldiers would have been housed in the buildings to the right and left here," Tessa explained. The duke and Lady Elizabeth had the main part of the castle to themselves. Wait until you see it. It's got—oh, there's no point in describing it. Let's just go inside." So they did.

There was a festive crowd gathering. The girls looked around at the others and were pleased to see that the costumes were about half Roundheads—looking very much like The Saddle Club, except, of course, they didn't have the nice room service menu masks—and half Cavaliers. The Cavaliers were all as glamorous as Tessa. Almost all of them had made an effort to assemble a costume in the style of the duke's time. Although Veronica, as usual, looked quite lovely, her outfit made her stand out in the crowd in a way she probably didn't like. That made Stevie very happy.

The duke's grand ballroom was spectacular. It was a large room, three stories high, completely surrounded by a balcony at the second story. Every inch of the room was festooned with ribbons and balloons in the duke's colors, red and white. At one end of the room, a platform held the orchestra. Lisa half expected to hear them play a minuet, but the music was modern—not exactly what the girls might have chosen themselves, but contemporary.

Stevie, Lisa, Tessa, and Carole began exploring the place. They wanted to know everything, and soon they did. They found a bar for the adults, but they also found a table with soft drinks for the young people. Caterers were setting out an enormous buffet to be served at midnight. The girls tried to figure out whether they'd go for the pasta salad or the dessert first.

"Dessert," Stevie said with conviction. To prove her point, she picked up a small cake that she didn't think anyone would miss.

Her friends shooed her away. They went back to the soft drink table and each took a glass of soda.

Stevie looked over at the entrance. "Well, look who's here!" she said brightly.

Lisa looked. It was the Italian boys, arriving together with their coach. Like the American girls, they were all dressed as Roundheads. Enrico looked very gallant. It nearly took Lisa's breath away.

Then she saw something that *did* take her breath away. While she and her friends had been exploring the ballroom, checking out the food and the drinks, Veronica had been waiting patiently by the door. The minute Enrico entered the ballroom, Veronica was there.

With a much practiced gesture, she flipped open a fan and began to agitate it in front of her flirtatiously. Enrico stopped to talk with her.

"She's like a spider, inviting the fly into her web, isn't she?" Lisa asked.

146

"Don't underestimate your friend, Enrico," Tessa said. "I think he can see right through her."

Lisa hoped Tessa was right. But she also knew that if Veronica was a girl who appealed to Enrico, then he definitely wasn't the right boy for her. She swallowed hard.

"Vould you like to dance?" a voice asked.

Lisa looked up, surprised. It was Henrik, the boy from the Dutch team.

"Well, sure," Lisa said, pleased and surprised. She found a place to park her cup of soda and followed Henrik out onto the dance floor.

For once in her life, Lisa was grateful to her mother, who had made Lisa take years of dancing classes—everything from tap to ballet, including ballroom dancing. Henrik's mother hadn't done the same. Lisa had to work very hard to keep him from stepping on her feet, but she knew what she was doing and she managed to preserve her toes and teach him something as they proceeded. Since Henrik's English wasn't very good, it was nice to be able to communicate as dance partners. When the music came to a stop, Lisa thanked him politely and returned to her friends. Henrik went in search of another partner. A few minutes later, Lisa saw him dancing with Ashley Hanna, who seemed very pleased by his attention.

"Hullo, fan club!" A voice greeted the girls brightly. It was Nigel.

They all gave him hugs and told him how pleased they were with his ninth-place finish for the day.

"I was rather pleased with it myself," Nigel said. "When Sterling has more experience on courses like that, he'll be bringing home blues."

"That's what he really needs, isn't it? More experience," said Lisa.

"Definitely," Nigel said. "He will certainly improve with experience. And, speaking of experience, I spotted an experienced dancer on the floor a few minutes ago." Nigel turned to Lisa. "Would you care to show me a step or two?" he asked, offering her his arm.

"My pleasure," Lisa said.

They walked out onto the dance floor. The music began and Nigel and Lisa started dancing. Within three steps, Lisa knew she was in the hands of a master.

"You're a great dancer!" she said happily.

"It's all rhythm and balance," he said. "All good riders are good dancers, too, don't you know?"

"I guess I do now," she said, relaxing to the music and enjoying the dance.

"Say, where's Lord Yaxley?" she asked after a while. "I thought a lord like him would want to be at this fancy ball."

"I don't think a lord like that wants to be anywhere near me," Nigel said. "He stormed off the castle grounds after Sterling and I finished the course. He wouldn't even talk to me. He just had his chauffeur leave me a message that he'd taken the noon plane back to London."

148

"What a sourpuss," said Lisa. "It's a pity he can't see all the wonderful qualities of his stallion."

"The only thing that man sees about Sterling is how much he paid for him."

"That's an awful way to think about an animal," Lisa said. "Yaxley should see the horse as an animal, not an investment. I wish he were here so I could tell him that myself."

"Well, I'd love to be there when you tell him that, but it's too late now. So, instead of talking about that foul man, I think you should just enjoy the evening."

"Perhaps," Lisa agreed. Then, without meaning to, she sighed. She couldn't help thinking about the terrible job her team had done that day. Even worse, she couldn't help thinking about Enrico, unable to resist Veronica's beauty, her fancy dress, and expensive jewels.

Enrico. How nice it would have been—

"Excuse me?"

Lisa was startled out of her thoughts. Nigel had stopped dancing and was turning around to talk to someone.

It was Enrico.

"May I dance with your partner?" he asked Nigel.

"I think she'd like that very much," Nigel said. He smiled at Lisa and gave her a little bow. "See you later," he said. Lisa was alone with Enrico on the dance floor.

"Shall we dance?" he asked.

18

THE MUSIC BEGAN. It was a slow song. Lisa felt her heart drop a little bit. When the music was quiet and slow, you were supposed to be able to talk with your dance partner. Lisa didn't have any idea what to say. Her mind filled with the image of Enrico chatting with Veronica at the stable, and as soon as that unpleasant picture melted, she saw Veronica welcoming him warmly at the door of the ballroom. He probably only wanted to dance with Lisa so he'd have a chance to explain that Veronica was going to be his new friend.

Enrico didn't say anything. He just held Lisa nicely as they moved to the music. But she could sense that he wanted to say something. That was what worried Lisa most.

Finally, he began.

"Your friend . . ."

"Yes?"

"That girl, Veronica . . ."

Here it comes, Lisa thought.

"Such a pretty girl . . ."

Lisa already knew that.

"Such an ugly heart."

"What?" Lisa said, surprised.

"All she wants to talk about is herself. I don't understand people like that. And the gaudy jewelry she was wearing . . ."

The meaning sank in. Enrico didn't like Veronica. He *really* didn't like Veronica. He hadn't fallen for any of her flirtations. He saw right through her.

Lisa felt a pleasant chill. Then she chided herself, wondering why it was she'd ever thought a smart guy like Enrico could be interested in Veronica. After all, the other night, they'd been laughing at Veronica's expense. Then Lisa told herself there was good reason she'd been nervous. Veronica was devious and unpredictable. She actually had the capacity to behave very nicely when it suited her. A lot of people couldn't see through the act.

"All she wanted to do around me was to show me how beautiful she is—and she *is*—and tell me that she's rich. She kept talking about jewelry, pearls, and diamonds. She talked about her jewels as if they were some kind of treasure. It was a lot of nonsense, if you ask me."

"Well, not exactly," Lisa said.

Enrico stopped dancing for a moment and held Lisa at arm's length as if to get a good look at her while he spoke. "What are you talking about?" he asked.

"Can you keep a secret?" she asked.

"With you? Certainly," he promised.

"Then let's start dancing again and I'll whisper in your ear."

Enrico took her back into his arms and once again they began dancing. As Lisa had promised, she whispered the entire conspiracy into his ear. He began laughing as he came to understand what Veronica's teammates were doing to her.

"The rhinestone from the button you picked up?" he asked in surprise.

"She believes it," Lisa said. "I mean it's only logical that a stone that had been buried for three hundred and fifty years might be a little damaged."

"Now that I think of it, when I told Veronica I was going to ask you to dance, she seemed very irritated. I thought she was angry with me, but then she said she had something important to do and she left the ballroom. Do you think she was going to go treasure-hunting by moonlight?"

"But of course!" Lisa said. "Moreover, if we've played our cards right, she's going to have a successful hunt." Then Lisa told him about the pyrite. "Want to go watch?" she asked.

"I wouldn't miss it for anything," he said, taking her hand and leading her out of the ballroom, through the courtyard, and into the open fields.

They stayed close to the castle walls, moving toward the oak tree. When they neared the tree, they could see Veronica scrambling in the dirt, holding her evening dress so that it wouldn't get too dirty.

"She's being so careful of her dress that I think she's hoping to find jewels she can wear back into the dance!"

"Shh," Enrico warned her, putting his finger gently on her lips.

They sneaked past Veronica and darted over to the stable tent, where they could hide behind the flaps of canvas. Behind them, they could hear the gentle snoring of 'Ank. It made Lisa and Enrico smile to know he was there, ever on the job. The horses seemed a little restless, perhaps from the long hard day they'd had. They were whinnying, snorting, stomping.

Under the tree, there was a flash of light. Veronica had apparently brought a penlight in her evening bag. The beam of light darted around the ground. Veronica reached out with her other hand. There was a tool in it, but it was too small to be the garden spade she'd used earlier.

"It's a spoon," Enrico told her.

"Sterling silver, I presume," Lisa said, giggling to herself. "She has to move a little more to the left—there she goes. . . ."

Veronica shifted to the left. Lisa held her breath. Veronica scratched at the earth with the spoon. The light held steadily. Then Veronica dropped the spoon and stood up, holding something in her hand.

"I think she's got it!" Lisa said.

Veronica opened her evening bag, dropped something into it, snapped off the penlight, and departed in such a terrible hurry that she left the spoon on the ground.

"Congratulations!" Enrico said, giving Lisa's shoulders a squeeze.

"What a team we are!" she declared. She offered her hand to Enrico in a high five. Instead of slapping her palm, he enfolded her upraised hand in his and then put his other hand around her back, holding her closely, warmly.

"Oh, Lisa," he said, almost sighing as he spoke. "You have so many sides to you that I keep discovering, and I find I like each better than the last."

Lisa felt just the same way. Enrico was warm, funny, talented, kind, a good friend, and a good rider. Moreover, he was about to kiss her.

"Four thousand miles," she said, uttering the thing both of them knew was true. They lived very far apart.

"Yes, but when we are together, the miles melt away. They do not matter."

And that was true, too. There, in the star-studded, moonlit darkness, Enrico looked deep into Lisa's eyes, and he began to reach for her with his lips and his heart.

Lisa's heart pounded with anticipation. It was as if all

her senses were turned on high. She could feel Enrico holding her, but she could also feel an encroaching warmth. She could hear his breathing, but she could also hear the horses on the other side of the canvas, now more awake than they had been before, neighing and whinnying with excitement.

She could smell the cool night and the pleasant clean scent of Enrico's aftershave, but she could also smell the presence of the horses, and there was something else, sharper, more acrid. Lisa couldn't identify it right then, but it would come to her. For now, there was Enrico.

She could see him, no longer dimly, in the darkness of the evening. It was as if there were another light, one behind her, a rich, warm, yellow glow, reflecting brightly in his eyes as they neared her own.

But it wasn't just a yellow glow. It was something else entirely. Lisa knew now what the smell was and why the horses were so agitated. She opened her mouth to say something—to tell Enrico. It took a moment for the sound to reach her throat.

"Fire!" she screamed as loudly as she could.

At just that instant, a bale of hay behind her burst into flames.

"WHAT WAS THAT?" Carole asked Stevie.

"What was what?" Stevie asked. "All I heard was the music. And it's not very good music, either, if you want my opinion. I think they should have gotten a band that could play something someone could *really* dance to, like—"

"I heard something. I know I did, and it sounded like Lisa."

"She and Enrico went out the door a few minutes ago. They had 'moonlight walk' written all over them. I doubt very much there's any screaming going on," Stevie said.

"Well, there is," said Carole with utter certainty. "Let's go."

The two girls hurried through the door of the ballroom

and out into the courtyard. It was deserted. Everybody was inside, dancing and having fun. Music, talk, and laughter came clearly through the doorway. But from the courtyard entrance, Stevie and Carole could hear another sound. It *was* Lisa and she *was* yelling for help.

"Fire!" Stevie repeated, deciphering the sound.

"Oh, no!" said Carole. "I'm going to the stable. You get help!" she said. Stevie spun around to go back to a telephone. Carole hurried to the stable.

The two of them ran as fast as they could, blessing the fact that they were sensibly dressed as Roundheads. Hoopskirts were no good in an emergency.

Carole assessed the situation quickly. Something was on fire in the tent. The tent itself must be made of fire-retardant material, but the straw and wood inside would burn furiously, endangering every horse inside. And, she knew, in a hot enough fire, anything would burn. There was no time to spare—soon the canvas would catch fire and collapse, trapping every living thing under a deadly blanket.

"Lisa! Enrico!" Carole shrieked.

"In here!" Lisa called back.

Carole found her friends frantically running from stall to stall, opening each one and trying to herd the horses out into the paddocks beyond. The noise, confusion, heat, and flames had awakened old 'Ank, and he was directing them.

"As long as the horses just leave, they'll be fine," Carole told Lisa. "Our job is to keep them from panicking."

157

That was easy to say and hard to do. Horses were prone to panic in unfamiliar situations, and they seemed to have a primal fear of fire. They knew it was dangerous and they wanted to run, no matter what obstacles—like other horses—might be in their way.

When Carole reached the tent, the fire was still relatively contained. But it was burning intensely and was about to spread. When it did, it would go from dangerous to deadly. There were only seconds.

'Ank pointed, telling Carole where to begin. She set to work.

She began opening stall doors and shooing horses out as quickly as she could, working toward the center of the fire so that she could help Lisa and Enrico where they most needed her, while moving the horses away from it.

Closer to the flames than Carole, Lisa pulled another stall door open. The bay gelding inside was terrified and didn't want to budge. Lisa's job was to make him want to move. She stepped in quickly, but not running. She didn't want to scare him more than he was scared already. She took him firmly by the halter and tugged gently, as if she were telling him it was time to go saddle up and compete. He reacted just as naturally, following her lead the same way he'd followed humans' leads from the first time a halter was ever put on him. As soon as he was out of the stall, Lisa gave him a gentle, encouraging slap on his flank. He knew what to do. He ran for safety.

"Next," she said out loud, trying to encourage herself.

Nearby Enrico was working silently, diligently, and efficiently. Open door, reach in for horse, lead horse out, move horse along. Next. With each horse, they came closer to the intensifying fire.

Lisa freed two more horses and then realized she was at the hottest part of the fire—near Sterling's stall.

The hay next to Sterling's stall was crackling in flames, and the blaze was spreading quickly. Right then, the fire was moving in the other direction, but Lisa knew that the slightest breeze would bring it right to Sterling's stall.

When Lisa saw the stallion, he was cowering in the back of his stall, as frightened as the bay she'd just freed. But he snorted and sniffed, and, smelling the sharp acrid bite of smoke, he was terrified into action. He whinnied loudly in protest.

"It's okay, Sterling. You're going to be okay, boy," Lisa said, pulling his stall door open.

She wished she believed her own words. Stallions were notoriously unpredictable and dangerous. A frightened stallion was treacherous. Lisa wouldn't be helping anybody if Sterling hurt her.

The smart thing to do would be to free another horse. There were many that only needed their stall doors opened and a little encouragement. She couldn't afford to waste time trying to save an unsavable horse.

Then Sterling rose on his hind feet, flailed his front feet in the air, and seemed to scream with terror. One look at the terrified stallion and Lisa knew she couldn't abandon him. She had to save him. She also knew she couldn't just walk into the stall. He could bludgeon her in an instant with one flailing foot. But, like the other horses, he was just waiting to be told what to do. The question was how to tell him so that he would understand.

"Lisa, you have to leave him!" Enrico said. "You can't save him if he won't save himself."

"I have to try," she said. "I just have to!"

A small flame sputtered to life in the straw near the open door of Sterling's stall. Lisa snuffed it out with her boot.

"Lisa!" Enrico said, now frightened for her safety.

She ignored Enrico's entreaty and turned around, trying to think what she could do. Then she saw a rope hanging on a hook and she knew the answer, but she couldn't do it on foot. She needed a horse.

Sterling's stall was at a place where two aisles came together. The Dickens horses were just two aisles over.

"Keep the flames out of here," she told Enrico. "I'll be back with help."

Enrico took off his jacket and used it to flail at the next outburst of fire.

Lisa ran to the Dickens stalls, grabbing the big circle of rope on her way. She threw open the doors of three of the stalls, freeing Miss Havisham, Copperfield, and Nickleby. She needed Pip for herself. The horse seemed to be waiting for her, ready to do as he was told. Lisa knew what she was going to tell him.

She opened his stall, hurried in, and pulled herself up onto his back. Then, without a bridle or a saddle, she rode Pip back to Sterling's stall. At first, Pip resisted, but he was well behaved and well trained. He was also a horse with an enormous amount of heart. Lisa knew that about him. If he could help, he would.

With only her legs on his belly and gentle signals on his neck, using his mane as a rein, Lisa got Pip to return to Sterling's stall.

Enrico was there, beating out the tongues of flame as they licked upward from the stall floor.

"Lisa, what are you doing?" he cried out to her when he saw her on Pip.

"I'm just a wild American cowboy," she told him. And with one swift motion of her right arm, she let out the lasso and began swinging the noose—just the way she'd learned to do it at Kate Devine's dude ranch. Enrico couldn't put out the flames anymore. Lisa knew that time had run out. She had one chance and one chance only to snare Sterling and run him to safety.

Enrico backed away from the stall. The lasso circled above Lisa's head, making a wide, easy arc.

"Now!" she said, and at that instant she freed the noose, sent it flying toward the startled stallion, and watched it settle over his head onto his neck.

"Yahoo!" she cried, tugging at her end of the rope to tighten the noose before Sterling found a way to shake it off. As soon as he felt the rope collar, he settled down. It

161

was just the same way the bay had relaxed when Lisa had tugged at his halter. The desire to please, to follow a human's instructions, was the foundation of a horse's training. Now it was saving Sterling's life.

Lisa tugged at the rope; Sterling followed. She and Pip led him out of the stable as fast as they could go. Enrico followed, running.

The fire was hot behind them, now burning completely out of control and spreading almost as fast as they could run.

In seconds, Lisa, Enrico, Sterling, and Pip were in the glorious freedom of the cool night air, safe from harm. Lisa unhitched the lasso from Sterling's neck and let him run free in the paddock. She slid down off Pip's smooth back and turned him out with his friends. Enrico took Lisa's hand and led her to the paddock fence. They climbed up, perching on the top rail to watch the flurry of activity around them.

Lisa was surprised to see all that was happening. She and Enrico had been so engrossed in freeing the horses that they'd been unaware of the arrival of the fire brigade and a hundred well-dressed volunteers from the costume ball.

Carole and Stevie found Lisa and Enrico and joined them on the fence. Together they watched. It was too late to save the stables. In a minute, the tent collapsed. But because Lisa and Enrico had been there and others had come quickly, not one horse was hurt. The fire brigade was able to contain the fire so that it never even reached the tack tents beyond the stable.

When the last flame was doused, Stevie said a most Stevie-like thing.

"I'm starved."

Lisa looked at her watch. It was five minutes to midnight. Almost time for the sumptuous buffet. She had just enough energy to race her friends back to the ballroom. The fact that Enrico held her hand all the way helped a lot.

20

THE BALLROOM WAS abuzz with talk about the fire, the fire brigade, and the miraculous facts that every horse was safe and the tack tent was untouched, thanks to the swift report of the fire.

As The Saddle Club, plus Tessa and Enrico, made their way to the buffet table, they heard snippets of the conversations.

"Can you believe it?"

"Some kids, I think . . ."

"That's what the fire marshal said . . ."

"An American girl it was . . ."

". . . three Americans."

"And an Italian boy," Lisa said, wanting to be sure that Enrico got credit.

She would have stopped to explain more thoroughly, but the delightful scents wafting toward her from the buffet table were too inviting. It was filled to capacity with the most delicious assortment of foods. There were trays of meats, vegetables, breads, and salads. It was hard to decide where to begin.

Stevie picked up a plate. She wondered if she could get everything onto one plate or if she should take two to begin with.

"Excuse me, miss," one of the caterers said politely. Stevie looked up at him. "There's a special buffet for the young riders."

He pointed. There, to the left, was a huge table filled with food specially prepared for the Pony Clubbers. Stevie blinked, wondering if she was seeing correctly.

"Pizza!" Lisa said, daring to utter the word first. Resignedly, the group headed for their own table and took a selection of the food.

A few minutes later, they were sitting in a circle, joined by the other young riders. Everybody at the dance had helped in one way or another to save the horses and put out the fire, but The Saddle Club and Enrico had been at the heart of it. The other kids wanted to know what had happened.

Carole told about Stevie's running for help. Stevie told about Carole's miraculously hearing Lisa's cries. Lisa told about Enrico's stamping out the fire. Enrico told about Lisa's saving Sterling.

"You what?" Stevie asked.

"I lassoed him, just like John Brightstar taught me."

"And you got him on the first try?" Carole asked.

"Yes, I did," Lisa said. "I've never done that before and I've been thinking about why it was I did it this time."

"And?" Stevie prompted.

"I think it was because I had to. There was no time left. If I hadn't roped him on my first try, he would have died in the fire. I knew it. So I did it."

"There you are, Lisa!" Nigel Hawthorne came over to the young riders. "I've been looking all over for you because I've just heard what you did for me."

"For Sterling, too," Carole said.

"For Sterling, definitely," Nigel said. "I can't believe how you managed to save the poor creature."

"I couldn't leave him," said Lisa. "You would have done exactly the same thing. Anybody would."

"Except maybe Lord Yaxley," said Nigel. "He's probably annoyed to know that Sterling was saved from near certain death. Just this morning, he was telling me that the horse was worth more to him dead than alive."

"That's a terrible thing to say," Lisa blurted out, setting her pizza down. "Why, that horse is so strong and so brave. All it took was just one little tug at his—what did Yaxley say to you?"

Nigel was a little surprised by the U-turn Lisa had made in her ranting, but he obliged her by repeating Yaxley's remark. "He told me the horse was worth more dead than alive. But surely you don't—"

Some things were becoming clear to Lisa, and at just that instant she saw something that made everything clear as crystal. A couple she'd never seen before walked past where the kids were sitting. The woman was helping the man because he was limping, favoring a leg that had probably got hurt while trying to rescue a horse.

"Oh, no," said Lisa.

"What is it?" Nigel asked, concerned by the look on Lisa's face.

"You said Yaxley left at noon, didn't you?"

"That's right. He told me he couldn't bear to watch any more of the cross-country competition and he was taking the noon plane back to London."

"But he didn't go back to London then," said Lisa.

"Of course he did," Nigel said.

"No. Seeing that man limp by just now made me remember that I saw Yaxley in a pub downtown this evening. He was having a beer with a man we've seen before. A man with a limp."

"Who?" Nigel asked.

"Him again?" said Stevie.

"*Who?*" Nigel repeated.

"The man with the limp," Carole explained. "We saw him hanging around the stables a couple of times. He was just sort of lurking. I didn't know he was a friend of Lord Yaxley's, though."

"Don't you see? 'Friend' isn't the right word," said Lisa. "What if he's not a friend and not a horse show fan? What if Yaxley hired him to start that fire? Both Enrico and I noticed that the fire definitely began right next to Sterling's stall. What if it wasn't just a coincidence? What if the fire was *started*—"

Stevie got the picture and finished drawing it. "—by a suspicious-looking man who's been lurking around the stables and hanging out and drinking beer with Yaxley. What if Yaxley just *said* he was going to London to establish an alibi because he'd already told Nigel the horse was worth more dead than alive?"

"Wow," said Carole. "How could anyone be willing to kill a horse?"

"He wasn't just willing to kill *one* horse," Enrico reminded the girls. "He only *wanted* to kill one, but he was *willing* to kill a stableful!"

"What do you think, Nigel?" Lisa asked.

"I think I'd better talk to the police," he said.

21

July 21
Cummington Castle

Dear Diary,

If there was any doubt in my mind about the duke's treasure, it was totally dispelled tonight. Tonight I found gold. It sits on the desk in front of me as I write, glittering temptingly.

I tried to call home to let them know what I'd found and to tell Daddy to be sure to arrange for the serious digging equipment—just because a few jewels have worked their way to the top doesn't mean the whole treasure is just inches below the surface. This will take some work. It will also take some experts, but Daddy can find those in Virginia.

The problem was that I could barely hear my parents and they could barely hear me. There was an incredible racket of sirens and horns going on outside. I yelled out the window for everybody to be quiet. Fat lot of good it did me. I may call again later tonight, but, now that I think about it, the telephone lines may not be secure. What if somebody overheard me? No, I guess I'll wait to talk to Daddy in person.

According to the Chumsuns, the duke was supposed to have a huge treasure chest filled to the top with jewels, dripping with pearls and diamonds—the biggest collection of wealth in England, next to the king. And soon it will be mine.

Oh, I know, you don't have to tell me. Any treasure we find will certainly be claimed by the British government, and they should get some of it. But there will be a reward. There definitely should be. I can see myself now, tea with the queen.

"Oh, it was nothing, Your Majesty," I'll say politely. But we'll both know better, won't we?

I will sleep well tonight and then I can spend tomorrow packing. I don't want to take a chance of missing the plane. I've just got to get home . . .

Veronica

"WHAT'S THAT BRIGHT light?" Stevie demanded, shading her eyes with her sheet.

"I'm afraid it's Mother Nature telling us that it's morning," Lisa said. She sat up in bed. "It can't be, though. It feels as though I just went to sleep twenty minutes ago."

"Shhhh," Stevie said. "If you keep on talking, you might wake me up."

"Stadium jumping!" Carole announced, sitting bolt upright.

"Wha?" Tessa asked sleepily.

"It's the last day of the competition. That means stadium jumping. Come on, we don't want to miss a minute of it." She glanced at her watch. "Hurry," she urged her friends.

"Hurry" was not in their vocabulary that morning. They had all been up until well past midnight. In fact, The Saddle Club had been at the police lineup for the man with the limp at two in the morning!

Lisa swung her feet out over the edge of her bed and prepared to stand up. "I still can't believe how quickly things happened last night," she said.

"Well, they did after you put everything together and told Nigel what had happened," Tessa said. "You'll go down in the annals of time as one of the world's great detectives."

"In this case, I think it would have been better if she'd figured it out before the plot got so thick," said Carole. "It was great to save all the horses. I just wish they hadn't been endangered in the first place."

Stevie sat up. "I'm awake," she announced. "But I'm not sure I'm happy about it."

171

"Welcome to the group," said Carole. She tossed Stevie's grooming clothes at her. "There's work to do."

They talked as they dressed. It gave them a chance to go over the night's events one more time.

"The police never would have found that guy if he hadn't been at the train station at one o'clock in the morning, waiting for the express train to London," said Lisa, tugging on her T-shirt.

"I still don't understand why he didn't drive," said Carole as she ran a comb through her hair.

"Oh, that's easy," said Tessa. "It's because he knew the train was faster. These old country roads are curvy and slow around the hills. The train goes right through them and is very direct. Feldman wanted to get to London before Yaxley listened to a radio and learned that all the horses had escaped alive. He had to collect the other half of his fee before Yaxley knew he hadn't earned it."

"Thank heavens he *didn't* earn it," Carole said. "All those beautiful horses!"

"Who's ready for breakfast?" Stevie asked.

"I am," Lisa declared. "Unless, of course, it's pizza."

Lisa wasn't prepared for what happened when they appeared at breakfast. There was a buzz of conversation in the dining room. Everybody was looking at The Saddle Club. (Stevie, Lisa, and Carole had unanimously agreed that Tessa should join, and she'd accepted their invitation immediately, so she was part of it now, too.)

"Everybody's looking at us," Lisa said.

172

"Everybody's trying to figure out which one of us is *you*," Stevie told her. "You're a hero, don't you know?"

"I don't feel like one," Lisa said. "I just think I did what I was supposed to do."

"Well, what one is supposed to do is to be a hero," Tessa explained. "But few accomplish it. Those who do are heroes. Ergo, you're a hero. Congratulations."

"Good morning, girls," Max said. "Did you sleep well?"

"Not enough," Stevie said, pulling out a chair at the breakfast table and collapsing into it.

"But enough to compete successfully today, I'm sure," said Max.

"Always enough to compete successfully," Stevie said.

The girls ordered their breakfast and drank juice until the food came. While they were waiting, Veronica appeared, refreshed and well rested. She joined the group at the table and gave her breakfast order to the waitress.

Tessa picked up the thread of the conversation they'd been having with Lisa earlier.

"Look, you may not feel like a hero because you just did what you were supposed to do, but while you were merely doing that, you were accomplishing a great deal. In a few brave acts you, first, discovered the fire; second, helped put it out; third, saved dozens of horses' lives—most particularly Sterling's life; and fourth, figured out what and *who* was behind the blaze. You *are* a hero, and I have little doubt that it will be recognized and acknowledged by many. I suspect you'll get a reward!"

173

"A reward? What are you talking about?" Veronica asked, paling at the word.

"Why, Lisa—for saving the horses last night," Stevie said.

"I beg your pardon?" Veronica asked.

"You mean you don't know?" Carole asked.

"Know what? What's this about a reward?"

Carole thought it was typical of Veronica that she'd find the idea of a reward more interesting than the idea that Lisa was a hero; that was Veronica and she wasn't about to change. What Carole had almost forgotten, however, was that Veronica hadn't been there at the fire. She'd been back at the hotel, following the wild-goose chase The Saddle Club had sent her on with the piece of pyrite. It was turning out better that any of them ever could have imagined!

Patiently Carole and her friends told Veronica everything that had happened the night before, being careful not to ask Veronica where she'd been.

It was fun to watch Veronica's face. It almost contorted. That gave Lisa particular pleasure because she was sure she knew what was going through Veronica's mind. Veronica was thinking how proud Enrico must be of Lisa-the-hero!

"Okay, girls, finish up," Max said when the story and breakfast had been finished. "We've got to get over to the castle and make sure the horses are ready for the final day of competition."

"Surely there won't be any riding today," Veronica said, astonished.

"Surely there *will* be," Max told her. "All the horses were saved from the fire, largely because of work done by your teammates. The tack and equipment are all in good shape. There's no reason not to ride."

Veronica pursed her lips. "I don't agree with that at all," she said. "I think the horses will be nervy and unpredictable. It can't possibly be safe to ride them today."

"The judges have announced that competition will go on as planned today for anyone who feels their horses are up to it," Max said. "The vet has already checked our horses and they are fine. The best possible thing for them is to get back to work. I think the same is true of the riders."

Veronica looked at him levelly. "I'm sure you think you're doing what's best for you, but I'm not sure it's best for me," she said. "I won't ride today."

With that, she rose and walked out of the dining room.

Max rolled his eyes. Then he looked over at The Saddle Club. "Does anyone know a qualified Pony Clubber who could join our team at the last minute?" he asked.

Four hands went up.

An hour later, the four girls settled in on the benches in the competitors' section at the show arena. There were eight challenging jumps set up in the ring, among them a tricky double and a very difficult triple jump combination.

At opposite corners, there was a large digital clock. Most of the time when The Saddle Club participated in jumping events, it was hunter jumping, where form and style were by far the most important and time mattered little. In stadium jumping, the only things that mattered were getting over without knocking anything down and speed. There were no penalties if the horse ticked the jump, only if the jump got knocked down. There were no extra points for grace and form. This was a race. It was an exciting event.

"That's what's great about a three-day event," Carole remarked, flipping through the program. "It tests so many different aspects of a horse's skills."

"The rider's, too," Stevie reminded her.

"Here comes the first competitor," said Lisa.

They watched carefully. It seemed as if only a few of the horses had clean rounds, meaning they rode the course without getting any penalty points. The girls were surprised by the course's difficulty.

They had an even bigger surprise when the PA system announced that the next rider was Nigel Hawthorne on Pound Sterling.

"He's riding today?" Stevie asked.

"I would have thought he'd be out of this, considering what Lord Yaxley did last night!" Tessa said.

"He's not doing this for Yaxley," Carole said. "He's doing this for himself and for Sterling. This is Sterling's best event."

Nigel and Sterling entered the ring. Almost everybody in the audience seemed to know who they were and what had happened. As the stallion trotted over to the judge's booth, The Saddle Club stood up to clap for their friend Nigel. The rest of the audience took that as a signal. Before they were even ready to compete, the audience gave them a standing ovation. Nigel tipped his hat.

The buzzer sounded. It was time for Nigel and Sterling to get to work. He turned his horse to go to the starting point of the course.

177

On the way, Nigel circled a few of the jumps at a trot, giving Sterling a little peek at them before he had to jump them. This also gave Nigel another chance to remind himself of the course and to be sure of his strategy.

Then, when they both were ready, the trot became a canter, Nigel crossed the line that started the clock timer, and they were off. Carole watched the horse's magnificent, muscular body propelling itself toward the first jump. The horse rose, passed over the obstacle, and landed as if the obstacle had never been there.

"What a jumper he is," she said. "For some horses, it's just in their blood." Her friends knew Carole was thinking about her own beloved Starlight, also a fine jumper.

The second jump was a double combination. Four jumpers in front of Nigel had knocked it down. Sterling soared over both parts of it.

The third jump was easier still for Sterling, and then came the triple combination—a killer for more than half the horses that had competed so far. It was as if Sterling never even saw it. He simply flew over all three fences. There was a gasp from the audience. A few people clapped. The others held their breath.

They needn't have worried. The rest of the course was as easy for Sterling as the first part. A total of 68.3 seconds after they began the course, they crossed the finish line.

"A new leader!" the PA system announced.

"Nigel's in first place!" Carole translated excitedly.

The girls clapped wildly. Nigel and Sterling got another standing ovation.

"Now *there's* a rider with fire in his heart," Tessa remarked.

The Saddle Club knew just what she meant, too.

23

AFTER THE JUMPING, the girls headed to the paddock designated for grooming for the day. Since there were no stables and no stalls, the competitors were coping with a makeshift setup. The horses didn't seem to notice the difference.

The lads offered to help, but all four members of the team wanted to do their own grooming and tacking up. Stevie, Lisa, and Carole were glad to know that Tessa agreed with them about that, too.

Max walked over to where they were working and nodded ever so slightly, indicating that he thought their grooming job was satisfactory. Then he started a pep talk for the team.

"You all know that I don't believe that winning is the

important part of competing. In fact, I think the only useful part of competition is that a worthy competitor makes you do your best. That's always been true of me and it's been true of every rider I've ever trained." He paused to point out some mud on Miss Havisham's fetlocks. Carole tended to it. Max continued. "However, I want to remind you that yesterday was not Horse Wise's finest hour when it comes to mounted games."

"You can say that again!" Stevie said.

"I hope I never have to say it again," Max said pointedly. Then he couldn't help himself. He started laughing, remembering the terrible mess they'd made of the games the day before.

"Don't worry, Max. We won't do that to you again," Stevie promised. "Look—here's why." She reached to pull something out of her backpack.

"What's that?" Lisa asked.

"It's a horseshoe," Tessa told her when Stevie held it up victoriously.

"It's not just *a* horseshoe," Stevie told her friends.

"It's the good-luck horseshoe!" Carole declared.

"You *stole* it from Pine Hollow?" Max asked, astonished.

"Borrowed, just borrowed," Stevie said hastily. "And besides, as long as you're here and it's here, it's still sort of with Pine Hollow, right?"

"Stevie, you know I *never* argue with you," Max said, trying to stifle a smile.

"Especially when I'm right," said Stevie.

Carole shook her head. There was nobody else in the world like Stevie, and maybe that was a good thing. Could the world stand two Stevies?

Tessa was mystified by all this. Lisa explained it to her. "Normally, this horseshoe is nailed to the door of our stable. Every rider has to touch it at the beginning of every ride. It keeps us all safe."

"No rider who has touched it has ever been seriously hurt," Carole told her. "It makes us ride carefully and well."

"But does it make us win?" Tessa asked.

"We'll see about that, won't we?" Stevie answered with a grin.

The girls finished their grooming, tacked up, mounted, and then warmed up their horses. Before they knew it, they were at the entrance to the ring. In turn, each of them touched the good-luck horseshoe, and then Stevie handed it to Max to hold while they went into the arena.

"Smile!" said the lady standing by the gate. They did.

Carole smiled not because the woman told her to, but because she was so proud and happy to be among the wonderful horses she and her friends had helped to save.

Stevie was smiling for more reasons than she could count before they got to their starting positions. She loved the fact that she'd convinced everyone she'd brought the good-luck horseshoe from Pine Hollow. The original was right where it belonged, nailed to the door of Pine Hollow on the other side of the Atlantic Ocean. The one Max was holding, which they had all just touched for good luck, was a twin that she'd found this morning among the burned rubble of the tent stable at Cummington Castle. She was also totally pleased that her prank on Veronica had been so successful that Veronica had refused to ride and they had Tessa as a teammate.

Lisa was happy in ways she had never known before. She was happy because of everything she'd been able to do the night before, and she was happy because a certain Italian boy seemed to think she was just about perfect. She couldn't stop smiling.

Tessa was smiling because she was happy to be with her friends.

When all the teams had lined up for the first race, the judge explained the rules. She had to do it carefully because this was an unusual kind of race. It involved water pistols and colored water.

The Horse Wise group looked at one another. This was exactly the kind of race they liked the best. It was just slightly crazy and right up their alley. More than that, it was almost identical to a horseback race Stevie had personally invented. She was right at home, and so were her teammates.

The handkerchief landed on the ground and Horse Wise was off. Lisa led. She dashed down to the far end of the arena, picked up the water pistol, and aimed, and a solid stream of green water found its mark right in the center of the target.

Next came Tessa. This sort of race wasn't as familiar to her as it was to the Virginia girls, but there was something infectious about their weirdness. She took aim with the red pistol.

"Bingo!" Stevie shouted proudly from the starting line, where she was waiting her turn.

Blue hit the target just as surely as green and red had done, and only a few seconds later Carole completed the picture with purple. First place. It made up for some of the misery they'd suffered the day before.

"Oh, I hope we don't have to carry eggs again," Carole moaned as they waited to find out what the second race was.

"I don't think so, and I'm getting a good feeling about this," said Stevie. She could see the judges dragging cartons of costumes to the finish line. Each player had to ride to the far end, dismount, put on a costume that consisted of pants, a shirt, and a hat, and then remount to return to the starting end. When the entire team was at the starting end in costume, they had to reverse the process, undressing at the far end.

"I think I invented this race, too," Stevie said.

"Well, if you didn't, you should have," Tessa said. "It's perfect for you!"

It seemed to be perfect for the whole team. Everything went absolutely smoothly, and they would have taken another first except for the fact that the British team was riding ponies instead of horses and they were easier to mount and dismount.

"Second place is good," said Lisa.

"First is better," Stevie reminded her.

"Two races to go," Carole said, bringing them both back to the present challenge.

The next race involved Hula Hoops. Each rider had to roll a hoop along the ground from horseback and then catch up with the hoop. Carole was grinning from ear to ear when she heard the rules of this one. Her father loved everything from the 1950s, and Carole had been raised with Hula Hoops. She could spin one with the best of them.

"It's all in the wrist," she told her teammates. "You flip it forward almost like a Frisbee, only, of course it's going to roll on the ground, not float in the air." She showed the girls what to do. They mimicked her gesture. "Perfect," she told them.

They did it pretty well, too. Horse Wise was neck and neck with the Italian team, vying for first place, when it was Carole's turn to do the final leg. In the lane next to them, Enrico took the Hula Hoop from Marco at the same instant Carole got hers from Stevie.

"Go for it!" Stevie called out to her best friend.

Carole did. She flipped the Hula Hoop twenty feet ahead of her, and it spun rapidly above the ground, spinning backward, so that when it touched the ground it seemed to roll back to Carole. Her pick-up was smooth as glass. Enrico had to chase his hoop all over the arena.

"Yoweeee!" Lisa yelled.

"Hip hip, hurray!" Tessa cheered.

Carole grinned broadly. They took another first place.

"The weirder the race, the better this team does, have I got that right?" Tessa asked.

"Perfectly," said Lisa. "See, when we do games at home, mostly they're ones Stevie invents. So we just got used to weird games. I hope this last one is the weirdest of all."

It was. It was almost too weird. The riders had to race to the far end of the course, eat a slice of pizza, and return to the starting area.

"We may have to disqualify ourselves," said Lisa, genuinely wondering if she could eat one more slice of pizza.

"We've got to do this for our Pony Club," said Stevie.

"Our stable," said Carole.

"Your country," teased Tessa. "I mean everybody thinks you Americans never eat anything but pizza and cheeseburgers. Show them they're right!"

"Okay," the Americans agreed.

And they did. The horses seemed inspired by the scent of the gooey cheese and tomato sauce. Pip even tried to take a bite of Lisa's pizza. She wouldn't let him have it. She thought it might not be allowed. She and her teammates did an inspired job of eating pizza. Even Tessa was good.

"Very good for a lady," Stevie remarked while she helped Tessa wipe the tomato sauce off her chin.

Then they all turned to cheer Carole across the finish line. She was still chewing, but the pizza was all gone and they'd come in first.

"I told you—it was the good-luck horseshoe!" said Stevie.

They were all sure she was right.

Then the judges handed out the final awards. The Saddle Club was afraid the ghastly day they'd had the day before would put them out of the running, but they'd done so well on the final day of the competition that they took an overall first. The Italians took second place; the British came in third; and the Dutch took a respectable fourth. Even though they were last, it was respectable because they'd worked so hard. The Saddle Club was glad they'd won, but they were even gladder that they'd had so much fun.

After the races were finished, the girls took their horses back to the paddocks and gave them a quick grooming. The Dickens grooms would pick them up later and take them home, where they'd get a more thorough cleaning. For now they needed hugs, treats, water, and rest. Each girl produced a couple of carrots and bid a fond farewell to the horse she'd ridden. Once again, they thanked Tessa for bringing the horses.

"We couldn't have won without them," Carole said, expressing the thought for all the girls.

"I don't know about that," said Tessa. "I think you're all wonderful riders no matter what horses you're riding." That made them give Tessa a hug, too.

They spent the rest of the morning watching the final riders in the stadium jumping competition. There were a lot of great horses and wonderful riders, but when all was said and done, Nigel and Sterling were very nearly the best. They took a second place.

"A perfect day!" Lisa declared when she'd finished clapping for Nigel. "Nothing could improve on it."

"Lisa Atwood? Miss Lisa Atwood?" Lisa looked around to see who was calling her name. People around her did the same.

"I'm Lisa Atwood," she said, identifying herself to a young woman in a business suit who seemed oddly out of place at the horse show.

"You? But you're just a girl!" said the woman.

"I guess I am," Lisa said. "Is there something wrong with that?"

"Oh, no," the woman said, blushing. "It's just that I was expecting—well, first let me introduce myself. My name is Sallie Latham. I'm from Equine Sureties. We're an insurance company for horses, many of the horses here, in fact, but most specifically, Pound Sterling."

"Did I do something wrong?" Lisa asked, afraid she might have hurt the horse.

"Wrong? Oh, not at all, my dear girl," said Sallie Latham. "You saved the horse's life and you saved a lot of our other clients' horses as well. I've come to give you a reward. From what I understand, you, personally, are the primary reason my company isn't paying out millions of pounds in claims today.

"Now, I've been authorized to give you this check, but I'm also authorized to take you and your whole party—all the brave young riders who helped—out to a celebration dinner tonight. Would you be available?"

Lisa looked around at her friends and all the other Pony Clubbers in the stand. "What do you say, guys? Are we free for dinner?"

"Absolutely!" everybody agreed.

"Good, then, it's set. I've reserved a room for our party at this wonderful pizza place . . ."

24

"OH, DEAR, WHERE are the boarding passes?" Max asked, shifting his raincoat from his right arm to his left and dropping a bagful of guidebooks at the same time.

"Your left inside jacket pocket," Lisa said.

"Your passports. What did I do with them?"

"You gave them back to us," Lisa told him.

"Then I guess it's time to go through security and get on the plane." Max and Mrs. Reg went first, followed by The Saddle Club. Veronica came last.

"After we go through security, I'm going to the first-class lounge," Veronica said. "I'll see you all in Washington."

"Grrrr," said Stevie, only somewhat under her breath. She was about to say something more loudly, but was stopped by the sound of a buzzer. Veronica had set off the alarm at the security gate.

"Please step back and empty your pockets," a guard asked her politely.

Veronica glared at the guard, but it didn't do any good. She had to empty her pockets.

The rest of the Pine Hollow group waited and watched.

Veronica reached into one pocket and removed a metal ashtray taken from their hotel. From the other she took an envelope. It was the hotel stationery, and it was sealed.

She walked through the security gate again and there was no buzz. She picked up the ashtray and put it back in her pocket.

"Open the envelope, please," the guard said.

"But—"

"Veronica!" Mrs. Reg said.

Veronica opened the envelope.

There, for all the world to see, was a "pearl," a "diamond," and a chunk of "gold."

"Oh!" said Stevie. "It's the fake pearl I lost from my necklace!"

"And there's the rhinestone from the button I found!" Lisa said.

"I never thought I'd see that chunk of fool's gold again!" Carole chimed in.

The Saddle Club grinned proudly, and at that instant Veronica knew she'd been had. Without a word, she turned on her heel and made a beeline for the first-class lounge, leaving the treasure behind.

"Pity the poor first-class flight attendants," Lisa remarked.

Max and Mrs. Reg tried hard not to laugh with The Saddle Club, but they couldn't help themselves.

"HELLO, DADDY? . . . It's Veronica . . . No, I'm calling you from the airplane. There's a telephone right here. Isn't that cool? . . . No, nothing's wrong, exactly. I just thought you should know that there was a little mistake . . . Right, well it has to do with those—the jewels, I mean, so maybe it would be a good idea if you canceled the order for the bulldozers . . . Not exactly. See, Daddy, well, it turns out that they aren't as precious as I thought . . . Actually, they were more like costume jewelry . . . Yes, I guess fakes is another way to put it, but there was no way I could tell, Daddy. Daddy? Daddy? Are you there?"

BEFORE LONG, THEY were halfway across the Atlantic, halfway home from a trip they couldn't believe was over.

"It was wonderful. I loved every single minute of it," said Lisa.

"Oh, you don't mean that," Stevie said. "Like you didn't really enjoy our second day of competition, did you?"

"Or risking your life to fight a fire that might have killed all the horses?" Carole reminded her.

"Well," Lisa conceded, "maybe not *every* minute. But it's nice to have that reward check—it's going straight into my savings account for a horse of my own. And I sure loved those last few minutes when Veronica realized that we'd fooled her about the duke's treasure."

"It would be nice if there were such a thing," Stevie said. "Can't you just see us all dripping in jewels and gold?"

Lisa looked out of the window of the plane for a moment, lost in thought. Then she turned to her friends. "Maybe we did find the treasure after all," she said.

Stevie looked for pearls and diamonds, but didn't see any. "What are you talking about?"

"It was something Tessa said about Nigel when he and Sterling were competing over the jumps. She said that he was a rider with fire in his heart. That was what the old guy—'Ank—said the legend was about. The treasure would be found by a rider with fire in his heart."

"You mean, like, Nigel got his treasure because he made Sterling perform brilliantly."

"Yes, that's what I mean," said Lisa.

"Then what about us?" Stevie asked.

Lisa knew she was still thinking about jewels, but she also knew that Stevie recognized a real treasure when she saw one. "For me, I think I had the most fire in my heart when I was in the middle of a fire and managed to lasso Sterling on my first try because I knew that was the only try I'd get. It made me feel better about myself than almost anything I've ever done."

Carole thought about what Lisa had said. "I felt good about doing such a wonderful job on the last day of the mounted games," Carole said. "It wasn't the blue ribbon. It was doing my best."

"And for me, I guess it was finding that the four of us—with Tessa, of course, not Veronica—could ride so wonderfully together," Stevie said. "What a team! There were other wonderful things, too, like the prank we played on Veronica and the good-luck horseshoe I found—"

"You *found?*" Carole said, echoing Stevie's words. "You mean that wasn't the real thing?"

"I thought it looked a little dirtier than I remembered," Lisa said.

"It worked, didn't it?" Stevie asked. They had to agree that it had. "So maybe it wasn't such a bad thing."

"Maybe," Carole admitted. She wasn't annoyed with Stevie. She and Lisa actually counted on Stevie to come up with silly things like that just when they most needed them. There was no point in being annoyed, especially when it *had* worked.

"Okay, so back to the fire in a rider's heart," Lisa said. "If I've got this right, we all think we had some of this fire, and in every case it had to do with riding and being with friends."

"And having fun and doing a good job and helping other people," Stevie added.

194

"So then it's clear to me what the duke's treasure really is," said Lisa.

"What?" Carole asked.

"The Saddle Club, of course," said Lisa. "It's the thing I care about the most."

"Me too," said Carole.

"Me three," said Stevie.

"One thing's for sure, then," said Lisa. "We've got the treasure and Veronica doesn't!" They gave one another a high fifteen.

The flight attendant interrupted their celebration. "Ready for lunch, girls?" she asked, lowering their tables to hold the trays.

"You bet!" Stevie said. "I could eat an elephant!"

"Sorry, there's no elephant on the menu—just a special selection for our young travelers: pizza!"

ABOUT THE AUTHOR

BONNIE BRYANT is the author of many books for young readers, including novelizations of movie hits such as *Teenage Mutant Ninja Turtles* and *Honey, I Blew Up the Kid*, written under her married name, B. B. Hiller.

Ms. Bryant began writing The Saddle Club in 1986. Although she had done some riding before that, she intensified her studies then, and found herself learning right along with her characters Stevie, Carole, and Lisa. She claims that they are all much better riders than she is.

Ms. Bryant was born and raised in New York City. She still lives there, in Greenwich Village, with her two sons.

READ ALL THE SUPER EDITIONS IN
BONNIE BRYANT'S EXCITING SADDLE CLUB SERIES!

A SUMMER WITHOUT HORSES

SADDLE CLUB SUPER EDITION #1

In this first super edition, there are three stories in one! When Stevie Lake injures herself and can't ride for a while, the other two members of The Saddle Club, Carole Hanson and Lisa Atwood, make a pact not to ride until Stevie has recovered. After all, they're The Saddle Club, and they always stick together. To seal the pact, the girls decide that if any of them break the vow, they'll have to ask stuck-up Veronica diAngelo to join their club. That'll keep them out of the saddle for sure!

But can three horse-crazy girls really stay away from horses and riding for more than a day? Find out in The Saddle Club Super Edition #1, which contains three separate stories about Lisa, Stevie, and Carole—and their summer without horses!

WESTERN STAR

SADDLE CLUB SUPER EDITION #3

The girls of The Saddle Club can't wait for winter break from school. Carole, Stevie, and Lisa are heading west to spend the first part of their vacation at one of their favorite places—the Bar None Ranch.

But what they thought would be a quick trip turns into a snowbound adventure. The girls must rescue a herd of horses that face a terrible fate. . . .

Join The Saddle Club on an unforgettable journey that recalls the true spirit of giving and the strength of friendship.